Praise for Robert B. Parker's
walking shadow . . .

Turn the page for more rave reviews . . .

P9-DCC-866

stardust

Spenser tries to protect a TV star from a would-be assassin . . .

"Classic Spenser . . . brilliant!"
—*The New York Times Book Review*

playmates

Spenser scores against corruption in the world of college basketball . . .

"A whole lotta fun . . . kick back and enjoy!"
—*New York Daily News*

perchance to dream

Robert B. Parker's acclaimed sequel to the Raymond Chandler classic, *The Big Sleep*, featuring detective Philip Marlowe . . .

"A stunning, drop-dead success . . . dazzling!"
—*Publishers Weekly*

poodle springs

Raymond Chandler's unfinished Marlowe thriller—completed by today's master of detective fiction, Robert B. Parker . . .

"A first-rate detective novel with all the suspense, action, and human drama that we have come to expect from the best."
—*Playboy*

WALKING SHADOW

ROBERT B. PARKER

BERKLEY BOOKS, NEW YORK

WALKING SHADOW

A Berkley Book / published by arrangement with
the author

PRINTING HISTORY
G. P. Putnam's Sons edition / May 1994
Berkley edition / June 1995

ISBN: 0-425-14774-6

BERKLEY®
Berkley Books are published by The Berkley Publishing Group,
200 Madison Avenue, New York, New York 10016.
BERKLEY and the "B" design
are trademarks belonging to Berkley Publishing Corporation.

PRINTED IN THE UNITED STATES OF AMERICA

10 9 8 7 6

acknowledgment

Most of what little I know of Chinese-American culture I learned from *Chinatown: A Portrait of a Closed Society,* by Gwen Kinkead. It is an informative book, and, even better, a great pleasure to read.

For Joan:

"Whom if ye please, I care for other none."

chapter
1

The last time I'd worked in Port City had been in 1989 when an important software tycoon had hired me to retrieve his wife, who had run off with a fisherman named Costa. Her name was, incredibly, Minerva, and I found her okay. She was living in a shack on the waterfront with Costa, who, when the fish weren't biting, which was mostly, worked as a collector for a local loan shark. This led Costa to believe that he was tougher than he actually was, a point he finally forced me to make. He spent a couple of days in the hospital afterward, and while he was in there Minerva refused to leave his side. I finally concluded that, despite his shortcomings, she was better off with him than she was with the important software tycoon, and I bowed out. The tycoon refused to pay me. And when I wouldn't tell him where his wife was, he attempted to get my license revoked. I heard that he went down to Port City himself after that and got booted out of town by the Police Chief, an ex-state cop named DeSpain, who as far as I could see ran the town, despite the official presence of a Mayor and a board of Aldermen. I called Minerva a couple of years later to see how she was, and they were gone. I never knew where.

Now, driving with Susan through a hard, cold rain that slanted in steadily against the windshield, nothing much had changed. The city was in a punch bowl, with the land sloping harshly down to the harbor. It had always been a fishing port, and once it had been a textile manufacturing city as well. But after the war, the mills had moved South in search of cheap labor. Now there was nothing but fish processing, and the smell of it hung over the town. In the time of the mills' flourishing, the Yankees who owned them had lived in handsome federalist houses up on Cabot Hill above the town, away from the smell of fish, and well clear of the fishermen and mill workers, and fish cutters living below them along the waterfront. They had founded a small liberal arts college, with a handsome endowment for the education of their children. They had played golf and tennis and ridden horseback and sailed twelve-meter sloops out of their yacht club at Sippican Point north of the city, where the water was still blue, and on clear days the sunlight skipped blithely along the crests of small waves.

When the mills moved out, Cabot Hill society staggered but didn't go down. It tightened in on itself, bought into the fish business, continued to be rich, added the Cabot academics to its ranks, and clustered around the college like survivors of a capsized boat clinging to a channel buoy. There was a neighborhood school on Cabot Hill and a brick-and-clapboard shopping center, where you could buy imported Brie and Armani suits.

There were two liquor stores, a movie theater, and a private security patrol with blue-and-yellow prowl cars. Who could ask for anything more.

The only reason to go downtown was the Port City Theater Company, of which Susan was a board member. The theater was connected in various ways to Cabot College. Its Artistic Director was on the Cabot faculty. The college subsidized it. And Cabot Hill was the prime source of its audience. The theater, which was in its fifteenth season of putting on plays too hard for me, flourished inscrutably amid the boarded-up store fronts, and the abandoned cars, near the waterfront. Which is where we were heading.

"How'd you end up on the board of a theater up here?" I said.

"Closest one that would have me," Susan said.

"And you want to be on the board because . . . ?"

"You know I love theater," Susan said. "It was a way to be involved."

"You're not contemplating a career change," I said.

"No. It may be a little late for that, and I love being a shrink. But it is a great treat for me to be involved, even peripherally, in the theater."

The rain was driven by a wind from the northeast, off the water. I had always speculated that the conjunction of hills and oceans produced more rain in Port City than anyplace else in Massachusetts. I had never gotten any support on that theory, but I stuck to it. Coming steadily in at us, staying slightly ahead of the wipers, the rain made the windows shimmer between wiper sweeps, and the oncoming traffic seemed a mirage through the sheeted rain water.

"What do you do?" I said.

"As a board member? Give money, raise money, and

lend high seriousness to the administrative proceedings of the theater."

"You don't make policy."

Susan smiled.

"This is true."

We were on the downtown side of Cabot Hill, the city itself below us, packed in along the waterfront looking prettier in the rain than I knew it to be. We passed a Cabot Hill Security vehicle parked at an intersection. I grinned.

"Beyond here there be monsters," I said.

"The line of demarcation is clear, isn't it," Susan said.

"Is it safe coming here to the theater at night?"

"There are always some of those private security people around. If you're really timid, you can park up on the hill in the shopping center, and the college provides a bus to bring people down from the hill."

"You probably don't park up on the hill and take the bus," I said.

"No."

"How did I know that?"

"As a . . ." she lowered her voice importantly . . . "board member . . ." her voice returned to normal . . . "I get to park next to the theater."

"This is a tough town," I said.

Susan shrugged.

Across the intersection the other Port City began. Three-decker houses lined the streets, so close together that you could barely squeeze down the tiny alley between them. On the steep hills the water in the gutters tumbled garbage along before it. Where the hills eased, the gutters were clogged and the rain water made deep puddles in the street, which overflowed onto the sidewalk. The rain had people off the streets, though occasionally I could see elderly Chinese people sitting on a roofed front porch, bundled in gray clothing, smoking and staring at the rain. We passed one of the empty mills, surrounded by gnarled and rusty chain link, the loading platforms sagging with decay, fork-lift pallets rotting on the frost-broken parking lot, surrounded with broken beer bottles and empty beer cans whose labels had faded into a uniformly faint yellow. There had been attempts to transform the vast brick hulks into other uses. The money had come from the hill, and the investors had put their money into things they would have liked if they had lived downtown. The peeling signs of artisan shops and blouse boutiques and yogurt shops and stores that sold antiques hung lopsided with age and weather, over the dysfunctional doorways. The mills remained empty.

"Isn't it ghastly," Susan said.

"Where late the sweet birds sang," I said.

Every few blocks there was a tiny store, dimly lit, with Chinese characters in the window. On another corner an old man in black pajamas huddled under an umbrella, selling something from a cardboard box between his feet. He had no customers as we passed. There were no dogs on the street. No toys in evidence. No children. No school buses. No automobiles parked by the curb. Once in a while a vacant lot, occasionally the rusting skeleton of an abandoned car, stripped of anything saleable. Everything sodden, under the downpour, narrow, bitter, and wet. Everything cooking sullenly with the slow fire of decay.

"Why such a big Chinese population?" Susan said.

"I don't know how it started, but they began to arrive here to work the fish plants. And others followed, and it grew like that. They work hard. A lot of them are illegal, so they don't complain about anything. They're suspicious of labor organizers and safety inspectors, and they take the wage you give them."

"A factory owner's dream," Susan said.

At the waterfront we turned left onto Ocean Street. Here there were no Chinese. Here the fishermen lived. There were more one-story homes, more room between them. But here too there was no sense that the rain was engendering. That it would bring forth fresh life. Here too the rain seemed almost pestilent as it bore down on the cluttered and makeshift homes that crowded against the slick ocean, where the greasy waves swelled against the waterlogged timbers of the fish piers. Almost the only color I had seen since I left the hill was the jewel-red stop lights gleaming through the murk at irregular intervals.

chapter
2

Demetrius Christopholous, the Artistic Director of the Port City Theater Company, was waiting for us, nursing a Manhattan, in the lounge of a Chinese restaurant called Wu's, a block from the theater. Susan introduced us. Christopholous glanced around the lounge, which featured a miniature bridge over a minuscule pond in the middle of the room. Muraled on the back wall was a painting of a volcano.

"The owner is on our board," he said.

"Is that a Chinese volcano painted on the wall?" I said.

Christopholous smiled.

"I think that's Mount Vesuvius," he said. "This used to be a pizzeria."

"Thrift," I said.

A disinterested waiter brought me a beer and Susan a glass of red wine.

"You're joining us tonight?" Christopholous said.

"Yes," I said. "Susan tells me you're being followed."

"Yes, of course, right down to business. It's quite distasteful, but that *is* why you're here, isn't it."

"I'm here because Susan asked me to come."

"Well, it's been a couple of weeks," Christopholous said. "At first I thought it just hypersensitivity on my part. One reads so much in the papers about these perilous times. But it soon became apparent that a person was stalking me."

"Can you describe him?"

"Always in black, at night, some distance away. He appeared to be medium height, medium build. Face was always shadowed by a hat."

"What kind of hat?"

"Some sort of slouch hat."

"Ever approach the shadow?"

"No. Frankly, I've been afraid to."

"Don't blame you," I said. "Person threaten you in any way?"

Christopholous shook his head.

"Approach you?" I said.

"No."

"Any harassment? Letters? Phone calls? Dirty tricks?"

"No."

"Any reason you can think of why someone would follow you? Disgruntled actor? Embittered dramaturge?"

Susan glanced at me. The "dramaturge" was showing off, and she knew it.

"The Artistic Director of a theater company has to make decisions that some people strongly feel are wrong," Christopholous said. "It is the nature of the work. But I can't imagine that anyone is acting out an artistic disagreement with me. Even if he were, why would he do this?"

"A lot of stalkers get a feeling of power," I said.

Christopholous raised his eyebrows and shrugged.

"Is that all they usually want? That feeling of power? Or do you think I'm in danger?"

"I can't say you're not. I can say that there has been no threat so far, which is good. But there's no way to say what will come. Have you talked to the cops?"

"No."

"Maybe you should."

"What can they do?"

"Depends on their manpower and their efficiency. They should have a stalker file, for instance. You might recognize a name. They probably could offer you some protection. They might be able to apprehend the guy."

"I'd . . . I'd rather this were a private matter."

"Why?"

"I . . . well, I'd like to protect the theater."

"Un huh."

We all were silent. I waited.

"And, ah, I, well I don't have much confidence in our police force."

"DeSpain still Chief?" I said.

"You know him?"

"I ran into him a couple times before," I said. "Once when he was a state cop, and once about five years ago when I was up here working."

"Yes, he's still the Chief."

It clearly made Christopholous uncomfortable to talk about DeSpain. I let it go.

"Any unresolved romantic complexity in your life?" I said.

Christopholous was glad to talk about something else. He smiled.

"No, most of that, for better or worse, is pretty well behind me."

"No ex-lovers that might want to follow you around?"

Christopholous smiled more broadly.

"No."

"Jealous spouses?"

Christopholous chuckled and looked at Susan.

"He's quite delicate for a man in his profession," Christopholous said. "He has phrased his questions without prejudging my sexual inclinations."

"Tough but sensitive," Susan said.

"Any jealous spouses?" I said.

"No. I wish there were."

"You owe money?"

"Just car payments. I make them regularly."

"What would you like me to do?" I said.

"Catch the shadow," Christopholous said.

"Okay."

"Do you think you can catch him?" Christopholous said.

"Sure," I said. "Him or her."

No sexist, I.

chapter
3

The Port City Theater Company was housed in what had once been the meeting hall of a church at the east end of a disgruntled avenue called Ocean Street. Behind it was a parking lot and beyond the parking lot the harbor where the water was iridescent with oil slick, and the loud gulls clustered to harvest the fragrant effluvia of the fish-packing plants. The church now housed some sleazy boutiques and cafés and places to buy theater memorabilia, and the hall, where once there had been bake sales, had been renovated by Cabot into a 350-seat theater. Christopholous left us in front and went around to the stage door.

"We gotta see this?" I said.

"Of course," Susan said. "I'm on the board. I can't come up here, have a drink with the Artistic Director, and not see the play."

"I can."

"But you love me," Susan said, "and you want to be with me."

"Of course," I said. "What's the play about?"

"Nobody seems to know."

"What do the actors say it's about?"

"They don't know," Susan said. She was as close to embarrassed as she gets.

"The actors don't know what it's about?"

"No."

"How about the Director?"

"Lou says that a play is not required to be about anything."

"And it runs how long?"

"Four and a half hours with an intermission."

Susan smiled encouragingly.

"It's very controversial," she said.

"Excellent," I said. "Maybe a fight will break out."

She smiled at me again, a smile perfectly capable of launching a thousand ships and very likely to burn the topless towers of Ilium. We got to the box office, collected our tickets, and went into the theater. The theater was full of people who lived on Cabot Hill and could trace their lineage back to the British Isles. It looked like a Cabot College faculty meeting. In a town fifty percent Portuguese and fifty percent Chinese, the theater was a hundred percent neither.

"I haven't seen so many Anglo Saxons in one place since the Republican convention," I said.

"You've never been to the Republican Convention," Susan said.

"I've never been asked," I said.

The houselights dimmed. The play began. On stage there were men dressed as women and women dressed as

men, and white people in blackface and black people in
whiteface, and a rabbi named O'Leary, and a priest
named Cohen. I knew the names because they were
printed on a big sandwich board which each of the actors
wore throughout the first act. There was someone in a
dog suit who kept saying *meow*. There was very little
dialogue, and the actors moved slowly about the stage
with angular gestures, stopping periodically in frozen
tableau, while an offstage voice recited something ominous that sounded like a hip-hop adaptation of *Thus
Spake Zarathustra*.

After an hour of this Susan leaned toward me and said,
"What do you think?"

"It's heavy-handed but impenetrable," I said.

"Not an easy achievement," Susan said.

The lead actor was in fool's motley, divided in two
vertical halves. One side was explicitly female, the other
side explicitly male. He/she came downstage and began
to speak directly to the audience.

"I am Tiresias," he/she said. "An old man with
wrinkled dugs."

He/she half turned and looked at a figure in some sort
of triangulated costume downstage left. The orchestra
suddenly began to play up tempo and he/she began to
sing.

"Lucky in love, lucky in love,
what else matters if you're lucky in love?"

The actor stopped. Simultaneously there was a flat
crack from the back of the theater. I recognized the
sound. The orchestra continued to play the accompani-
ment. The actor took a silent step backwards and a red
stain began to soak through the costume. I got up and

started for the stage as the actor sank to his knees, and then fell backwards onto the floor, his legs bent partially back under him. Still the audience didn't get it. The other actors were motionless for a moment, and then one of them, a tall actress in blackface, lunged forward and dropped to her knees beside the actor just as I reached them.

There were people standing in the wings. I shouted at one of them.

"Call 911," I yelled. "Tell them he's been shot."

I felt for the actor's pulse. I couldn't find it. I tilted his head, blew two big breaths into his mouth.

"You know CPR?" I said.

She shook her head. I pushed her gently out of the way with one arm and started chest compression. The front of his shirt was slick with blood. A pair of tan slacks appeared beside me as I pumped his chest. Allan Edmonds loafers. No socks.

A voice said, "I'm a doctor."

"Good," I said. "Jump in."

He said to someone, "Get me something, towels, anything."

He said to me, "Pulse?"

"No," I said.

I saw his hand reach in and take the actor's arm and feel for the pulse in his wrist and hold it, feeling. Then some towels came into view and he said, "Stop for a minute."

I did. He ripped down the front of the actor's shirt and wiped the chest with a folded hand towel. There was a small entry wound, directly over the heart. The flesh was puffed slightly around the edges of the puncture, from which the blood welled as fast as he could wipe it away.

"Shit," he said, and folded the towel one more time and put it over the wound.

"A rock and a hard place," the doctor said. He seemed to be talking to himself more than to us. "The chest pressure will increase the bleeding, but if his heart isn't started he's dead anyway."

"Bullet should be right in his heart," I said, between breaths. "Given the location of the entry wound."

"Probably," the doctor said. "Which makes it pretty much academic."

He paused for a moment. Then he shrugged.

"It's the best we can do," he said.

"He's not going to start up," I said.

"I know," the doctor said.

But we kept at it for what seemed forever—long after the actor was gone, long after anyone thought he wasn't.

The ambulance arrived and the EMTs took over the futile effort. I stood up feeling a little dizzy, and realized that the theater was still full, and entirely silent. The cast ringed us in a motionless circle. Susan had come up on stage, and a nice-looking, black-haired woman wearing a big diamond and a wedding ring was standing by the orchestra pit, apparently waiting for the doctor. Two Port City cops had arrived. One cop was talking into his radio. Soon there'd be many cops.

"Any chance?" Susan said.

I shrugged.

"He's got a hole in his heart," I said.

Susan looked at the doctor. He nodded.

"Not my specialty," he said. "I'm an orthopedic surgeon. But I'd say he was dead when he hit the floor."

I looked at the tallish actress standing beside us in her ridiculous black makeup. Her face was vacant. The pupils of her eyes seemed big.

"You okay?" I said.

She shook her head. More cops arrived. Uniforms and lab guys and detectives. I recognized DeSpain.

"I know you," he said.

"Spenser," I said. "How are you, DeSpain."

"You used to work out of the Middlesex DA's office."

"Long time ago," I said. "I'm private now."

DeSpain nodded.

"You did some work up here five, six years ago," DeSpain said.

He looked at the doctor.

"Who's this," he said.

"Steve Franklin," the doctor said. "I was in the audience—I'm an MD."

DeSpain nodded. He was a big blond guy with bright blue eyes that seemed to have no depth at all.

"DeSpain," he said. "I'm Chief of Police here. He going to make it?"

"I don't think so," the doctor said.

DeSpain looked back at me.

"So," DeSpain said. "Tell me about it."

"Shot once," I said. "From the back of the theater. I didn't see the shooter. Probably a .22 from the sound and the entry hole, maybe a target gun. It was a hell of a shot. Right through the heart."

"The killer may know something of anatomy," the doctor said. "Most people don't know exactly where the heart is."

"A good shot that knows anatomy," DeSpain said as if to himself. "Hell, we've got the bastard cornered."

We got out of there very late in the evening, and drove Christopholous home. He lived on the first floor of a two-family house next to a Chinese market, across the street from a fish-processing plant.

"Can you help us on this?" Christopholous said when I parked out front.

"The murder?"

"Yes."

"I can't catch your shadow at the same time," I said.

"Do you think they're related?"

"I hate coincidences," I said.

"I . . . think the murder takes precedence," Christopholous said.

"Would you like to know my rates?"

"I thought . . . we don't have any money . . . I was hoping, as a friend of the theater . . . ?"

I looked at Susan.

"My usual fee?" I said.

"I'll double it," she said.

"Okay," I said to Christopholous. "I'll watch you to your doorway. When you're inside, lock it. If someone wants in, be sure you know who you're opening it for."

"You think I'm in danger?"

"There's some around," I said. "What time do you leave your house in the morning?"

"Nine o'clock, usually. I stop off and have coffee, and get to the theater around ten."

"Someone will pick you up," I said, "and keep an eye on you and see if the shadow's around. Probably be a black man about my size but not as good-looking."

Christopholous nodded. He hesitated, then shrugged and got out of the car. I watched him climb the front steps and go into his shabby house and close the door. In a minute, lights showed through some windows to the right of the doorway. I pulled away.

On the ride home, Susan said, "Remind me again of your usual fee?"

"Two nights of ecstasy."

"So doubled would be four," Susan said. "Payable in thirty days?"

"Normally, but doubling the amount includes halving the time."

"So four nights of ecstasy in two weeks," Susan said. "That's the deal?"

"Yes."

We were quiet rolling through the empty darkness north of Boston. Susan giggled.

"Sucker," she said.

"You don't think I'm charging enough?" I said.

"It's enough," Susan said, "but you'd have gotten it anyway."

"I know."

chapter
4

Most people having dinner Upstairs at the Pudding had never seen anyone who looked like Hawk. At 6′ 2″ he weighed 210 and had a 29-inch waist. He was monochromatic tonight. Black skin, black eyes, black suit, black shirt, black tie, black boots. His head was clean-shaven.

"This place is so Cambridge," Susan said, "it gives me goose bumps."

"Cambridge give you goose bumps?" I said to Hawk.

"Hives," Hawk said.

The main dining room had a thirty-foot ceiling, and the dark green walls were decorated with posters advertising Hasty Pudding Club productions dating back to the early nineteenth century. We sat at a table outside on the patio deck.

"Think maybe I'm integrating the place?" Hawk said.

"You're so sensitive," Susan said. "There was a Kenyan diplomat in here just last year."

Hawk grinned.

"Don't smile," I said. "Ruins the look."

Susan was busily waving at people.

"You're like the Mayor here," Hawk said.

"And rightly so," Susan said.

The waitress came and took our order.

"Well, nobody following your Greek," Hawk said. "I been on his tail since you called me."

"You think the shadow saw you?" Susan said.

Hawk stared at Susan as if she'd spoken in tongues.

"I beg your pardon," Susan said.

"Sure," Hawk said. "Could mean the shadow heard about me."

"Which would make him likely part of the theater company, or at least someone in Christopholous' circle," I said.

"Un huh. Or the murder stirred everything up and scared him off," Hawk said.

"Or?"

"Or Christopholous made him up," Hawk said.

"Or her," Susan said.

Hawk and I both smiled, and nodded.

A young couple with a baby stopped at our table.

"This is my friend, Diane," Susan said. "And her husband, Dennis. And their daughter, Lois Helen Alksninis."

Hawk put his finger out and the baby grabbed it.

"Name's bigger than the kid," Hawk said. "What kind of name is that?"

"A hard one," Dennis said and Hawk grinned. Lois Helen let go of his finger. And they moved on to their table.

"Did you speak to that policeman?" Susan said.

"DeSpain? Yeah. I went over this morning."

"DeSpain?" Hawk said. "State cop? Big blond guy, stone eyes?"

"Yeah," I said. "Except now he's Chief in Port City."

"Port City a tough town," Hawk said.

"I know."

"DeSpain a tough guy," Hawk said.

"What a coincidence," I said.

A lean, outdoors-looking man in a blue blazer passed us on his way to the door. He saw Hawk and nodded slightly. Hawk nodded back.

"Who's that?" Susan said.

"Hall Peterson," Hawk said. "Do some investments for me."

"Investments, Hawk?" Susan said. "You never cease to amaze."

"Never," Hawk said.

"Victim's name was Craig Sampson," I said for Hawk's benefit. I looked at Susan. "What do we know about him?"

"He was forty-one, forty-two," Susan said. "Single. Poor family. Never went to college. He went to acting school at night on the GI Bill, or whatever they call it now, and waited on table, and worked for a caterer, and for a home cleaning service, and painted apartments, and lived in hideous little one-room walkups downtown in New York, and all the other awful stuff you do if you want to be an actor, and finally he auditioned for the Port City Company last year and made it."

"That's all?"

"Doesn't seem like much, does it," Susan said.

"Not going to be more," Hawk said.

Susan nodded. Hawk and I were quiet. There were

trees growing up around the patio dining room, and plants along the railing. There was no roof. The effect was of dining in a private treehouse in a lush garden, although we were twenty feet up from Harvard Square. Overhead, small lights strung along the beamed superstructure twinkled like captive stars, above them the darkness ascended infinitely. I looked at Susan across the table. Her eyes seemed as deep as space; and I felt, as I always did when I looked at her, as if I were staring at eternity. I half expected Peter Pan to cruise in and make me young again.

"You want me to stay on the Greek?" Hawk said.

"Christopholous, yes."

"And if I see a shadow you want me to grab him . . ." he looked at Susan . . . "or her?"

"It would be nice if we could chat with him . . . or her."

"What you going to do?" Hawk said.

"Susan and I are going to a reception and board meeting at the theater," I said.

"What could be better," Hawk said.

"How about getting whacked in the nose with a brick?" I said.

"Well, yeah," Hawk said. "That would be better."

Susan gazed up at the night sky.

"One and a half billion males on the planet and I'm having dinner with Heckel and Jeckel," she said.

The entrées arrived. Susan cut her tuna steak in two and put one half of it aside on her butter plate. Hawk watched her.

"Trying to lose some weight?" Hawk said in a neutral voice.

"Yes. I have three or four pounds of disgusting fat that I want to get rid of."

Hawk said, "Un huh."

"I know, maybe you can't see it, but it's there."

Hawk looked at me.

"I've missed it too," I said. "And I'm a trained detective."

"Remember where we are," Susan said. "I could have you both arrested for sexual harassment."

"I counter with the charge of racial insensitivity," Hawk said.

"Yes," Susan said. "That would be appropriate. Then we join forces against our common oppressor."

They both turned and gazed at me.

"The white guy," I said.

chapter
5

Susan and I met Christopholous in the conference room upstairs, where board members and invited guests milled thirstily around the open bar.

"Please call me Jimmy," Christopholous said. "It's the English version of Demetrius. I try not to be too ethnic."

"Christopholous kinda gives it away though," I said.

He smiled.

"Well, all one can do is one's best," he said. "Thank you for agreeing to meet with us. I've not seen your black man."

"He's been there," I said.

"Really? He's very elusive."

"So's your shadow," I said. "There's been no sign of him."

"Perhaps this terrible business has frightened him

away," Christopholous said. "Susan, you look as radiant as you always do."

"It's the board meeting," she said. "I get so excited."

"Of course," he said and turned to an older woman in a flowered dress and took both her hands in his. Susan and I moved away.

"Trying times, Dodie, trying times. You look radiant, anyway, as you always do."

We were in a meeting room upstairs from the theater having cocktails and buffet. The room was crowded with board members, members of the acting company, directors, stage managers, set designers, important guests, like me, and assorted kids from the caterer in tuxedo shirts and cummerbunds moving adroitly through the jam, passing trays of hors d'oeuvres. I saw the tall actress, who had been next to Craig Sampson. I smiled at her. She nodded.

"What's her name?" I said.

"Jocelyn," Susan said. "Jocelyn Colby."

I got a beer from the bar set on a table in front of the windows. Around the walls of the conference room were galleried posters of past theatrical productions: two swordsmen in Elizabethan dress; a partially dressed woman bound elegantly to a chair; the backlit outline of two people, heads close together, framed by a gigantic white moon; a white horse's head, nostrils distended, eyes wild, against a black background. The posters paraded in several rows along every wall. En masse they were diverse and yet the same; all had the theater poster look. I mused on what that was for a while until I had drunk my beer. Then I stopped thinking about the order and diversity of theatrical posters and, instead, thought about getting another beer. I decided in favor of it, and did.

"Do they usually have the actors come to the board meetings?" I said with my new bottle of beer cold in my grip. I tried to hold it lightly so as not to warm it with my hand.

"There's usually a few to shmooze the board members. Tonight is special though."

"Because I'm here?"

Susan smiled.

"That's always special, don't you think?"

A young woman with big hair came to stand directly in front of me. She had a chest in which she took obvious pride.

"Susan," she said. "Is this him? I've got to meet him. Isn't he big?"

Susan smiled and introduced us. The young woman's name was Deirdre Thompson.

"Are you a member of the company?" I said.

"Yes. But I'm thinking of going to L.A. after this season. Do you carry a gun?"

"Force of habit," I said. "I don't really need it when Susan's with me."

Deirdre looked back at Susan and pumped her fist.

"Way to go, Susan," she said. "Hunk city."

Then she turned away and moved off into the crowd, looking for a drink.

"Do you think she has designs on me sexually," I said.

"Almost certainly," Susan said.

"Is it because I'm hunk city?"

"It's because you're male."

We moved through the pack, trying to find a space I would fit into. Along the way, Susan introduced me. "Myra and Bob Kraft—Foxboro Stadium . . . Jane Burgess, she works out with me at Mt. Auburn . . . Rikki Wu, we had a drink at her restaurant Tuesday night."

"My husband's restaurant," Rikki Wu said. "I really have no head for business."

"And probably don't need one," I said, just to be saying something.

"You're very kind," Rikki Wu said. "I'm delighted finally to meet the mysterious boyfriend."

I smiled. Susan smiled. We moved on.

"Is everyone underdressed but Rikki?" I said.

"No," Susan said. "Here's Dan Foley."

Susan introduced us.

"You here alone?" I said.

He shook his head.

"Too bad," I said. "I was going to point you at Deirdre."

Dan moved away, toward his wife. We reached the buffet table. There was shrimp cocktail, and black bean salad, chicken saté, cold sliced tenderloin, spring rolls, and lobster medallions with avocado.

"Will I lose credibility with the board," I said, "if I slobber black bean salad on my tie?"

"Absolutely."

"On the other hand," I said, "maybe they'll be so excited to meet the mysterious boyfriend, they'll probably forgive me any indiscretion."

"Probably."

We ate. Or to be accurate, the board guzzled, I ate, and Susan nibbled. Finally when there was nothing left to guzzle, eat, or nibble, the members of the board gathered reluctantly around a big table in the boardroom, and the meeting started. The actors and others from the company stood against the walls.

"Thank you all for coming," Christopholous said and waited a moment until the small talk subsided. "We had

originally scheduled a presentation by the capital acqui-
sition committee on our fall event."

Everyone was quiet. In fact one guy with a bright red
face looked as if he might be resting.

"But in light of our horrible tragedy this week, I have
taken the liberty of postponing that, and of asking all
members of the theater family to come together tonight
to discuss the tragedy. I know many of you met tonight's
guest at the reception, but for those who didn't . . ." He
gestured toward me somewhat theatrically, I thought. On
the other hand, we were in a theater.

"Mr. Spenser is a professional detective," Christopholous said. "And, in a sense, a part of the Port City
family, being the very special friend of our wonderful
events chairman, Dr. Susan Silverman."

Susan glanced at me and said *Shut up,* soundlessly.

"Mr. Spenser initially came to us via Susan, in regard
to a stalking incident. He is a former police detective,
now in private practice. And he has agreed to provide
professional counsel in this dreadful business. Mr. Spenser,
perhaps you could initiate the discussion."

I felt like I should have a pointer. I stayed seated.

"This may not be a routine murder," I said. "Most
murders don't happen in a crowded theater, for instance.
But if it turns out to be motivated by the routine
things—love and money—then the cops probably will
do better with it than I can. They have manpower. But
they also have other things to worry about. And if this
doesn't solve quickly, they will get distracted. I won't.
What I can do for you is worry about this exclusively."

Rikki Wu raised her hand. She looked about forty,
wearing a tight little black dress, sapphire earrings, a
sapphire and diamond necklace, and a wedding ring with
a diamond as big as the Ritz. She was expertly made up.

Her mouth was wide. She had big, dark eyes. And she appeared to take excellent care of herself.

"Yes, Ma'am."

"Are any of the rest of us in danger?"

"I don't know," I said.

"What are you going to do about that?"

"Try to catch the killer."

"How can we help?" she said.

"Tell me what you know," I said.

"I don't know anything."

I smiled at her.

"Don't be so hard on yourself," I said. "Was there any love interest in Craig Sampson's life?"

"I wouldn't know," she said.

I looked at Christopholous. He shook his head.

"Girlfriend?"

Christopholous shook his head.

"Boyfriend?"

"I don't know," Christopholous said.

Rikki Wu frowned. Things were moving too fast for her.

"I don't see why you're asking these questions. Are you implying that Craig was gay?"

"I'm asking," I said.

"Well, why are you asking? What has that to do with his death?"

"I don't know," I said. "I don't know if he's gay. I don't know if his sexuality had anything to do with his death. If he has a boyfriend or a girlfriend they might be someone I should talk to. If he has neither, why not?"

Rikki Wu was spirited.

"Well, I think it's none of your damned business," she said.

"Yeah, actually, it is. This is a murder investigation.

We don't know anything but the fact of the murder. We have to find out everything else, and the way to find it out is to ask questions. I have no facts. I'm looking for facts. So I ask questions. Eighty, ninety percent of the facts you get by asking questions are probably useless, but there's no way to know that except to ask."

"Well, I think you are going about it very crudely."

"After you talk to DeSpain, you'll think I was Jascha Heifetz," I said. "How about money? He in debt? He have a lot?"

Nobody had anything to say.

"Dope?"

Rikki Wu had had enough.

"This is indecent," she said. Her face was flushed and her eyebrows were drawn down into the kind of pretty frown that had doubtless gotten her the diamond.

"Poor Craig is the victim. You act as if he were the guilty party."

"Oh, for crissake, Rikki," Susan said. "People are usually killed for reasons. Those reasons often have to do with sex and money."

"Well, I don't like it," Rikki said.

Her shiny lower lip was pushed out slightly, which meant I was supposed to jump across the table and lie on the floor at her feet. I assessed the table and decided it was too wide.

Susan said, "This is not about you, Rikki."

Rikki looked startled.

"I don't wish to talk about it," Rikki said. "Jimmy?"

Christopholous had been gazing off into the middle distance, probably thinking about the late plays of the Wakefield Master. He refocused slowly and smiled lovingly at Rikki Wu.

"Darling," he said. "You should do whatever you want to do."

"I'm leaving," she said.

"Oh, Rikki," Christopholous said, "don't do that. We'll all be devastated. Somebody, get Rikki a lovely glass of champagne."

Somebody offered her a glass. The storm passed. Rikki smiled at Christopholous, accepted her lovely glass of champagne, and tacitly agreed to stay through the meeting. The red-faced guy who had been resting his eyes let out a sort of blubbery snort and his head jerked and he looked a little puzzled for a moment about where he was. He spotted his champagne glass, still partially full, and picked it up and drained it, then he settled back in his chair and tried to look as if he knew what was going on. It was a look I had often worked on myself.

"Okay," I said. "Here's another question. What the hell was the play about?"

There was the usual silence.

"It's not a frivolous question," I said. "The killing could be connected to the play."

"That's ridiculous." It was Lou Montana, the Director, portly and red, wearing a safari jacket.

"An actor getting shot on stage while wearing motley and singing 'Lucky in Love' is ridiculous," I said.

"Well, what was *your* response to the play?" Lou Montana said, and his voice was ominous. He must have scared hell out of the apprentice actors.

"I thought it a pretentious mishmash about appearance and reality."

"Art is not 'about' anything," Lou said tiredly, putting large verbal quotation marks around the *about*. "It is movement and speech in space and time."

"Thank you," I said.

"I didn't expect you to understand," Lou said.

"Me either."

It went like that for the rest of the evening. The board was *important*. And it was determined to prove it to me. Mercifully, the wine ran out before I did, and the meeting ended. I didn't know anything I hadn't known before. Maybe less.

We held hands as we walked to our car. The wet-empty street was implacably seedy in the unforgiving glare of the mercury street lamps. Susan glanced up at me with a smile.

"You don't want to take the security bus up the hill?" Susan said.

"I'm armed," I said. "Let's risk it to the car."

As we walked, Susan bumped her head gently on my shoulder. I heard her laugh a little.

"What's funny," I said.

"Jascha Heifetz?" she said.

I shrugged.

"Sometimes I say Yehudi Menuhin."

chapter
6

Christopholous' office was mostly blond wood and exposed red brick. The laminated ceiling beams, the window casements, and the wide-board yellow pine floor were all stained about the color of a palomino horse. Christopholous sat behind a mission oak desk that matched the rest of the room. He was wearing a tweed jacket, and his wide, round face above the graying beard was tanned and healthy-looking.

"First let me apologize for the board," Christopholous said.

"Being smart isn't always the primary function of a board," I said.

Christopholous smiled.

"Quite true," he said. "Willingness to raise or donate money counts for a lot."

"Counts for approximately everything, I would think."

Christopholous kept his smile but made it wry.

"The arts are a very precarious proposition these days. Reagan and Bush killed us. And dear Jesse Helms, who suspects *Little Women* of having a lesbian agenda."

"Grants dried up, have they?"

"In the name of thrift," Christopholous said. "They still subsidize fucking tobacco, which is a fucking poison, excuse my French, but they save money by cutting back on the arts."

"That's 'cause they don't grow arts in North Carolina," I said.

"Sure, I know that. But they pretend to believe that theater and other performing arts should be self-supporting. For crissake, Shakespeare was subsidized. If the performing and visual arts must support themselves, then they will be required to be popular. Television is what you get when you try for commercial art. Plays like *Handy Dandy* would never be put up."

I smiled.

"I know. You feel that would be no loss. To tell you the truth, and I'd deny publicly that I ever said this, I don't like the play either. But it is an attempt to grapple artistically with some fundamental issues, and, however clumsily rendered, it is an attempt that needs to be encouraged."

"Especially when you've got a hole in your schedule," I said.

"Especially then. I'm not a holy person. Had there been a better play available, we'd have put it up. I'm trying to make a living, and see to it that the company makes a living, and draw an audience, and raise money to make this thing work. It means I put on things I don't like, and kiss asses, and tolerate ignoramuses. On the other hand, we don't have *Cats* in for an extended run."

"That's something to be grateful for," I said.

"Real theater, any art, speaks the otherwise inarticulate impulses of the culture," Christopholous said. "Art energizes the collective consciousness. The arts are more vital to the well-being of a society than missiles or Medicare. Do you know that English theater grew out of early religious ritual?"

Christopholous was a hyperbolic shmoozer, and a remorseless fund-raiser, and he made me tired. But he was also one of the major thinkers about theater in the world. I had read a couple of his books, and the voice from the books was the voice he was using now.

"Quem Quaeritis," I said.

I was showing off again, like when I'd said "dramaturge." And it worked again. Christopholous looked at me as if I had just levitated.

"You are an odd goddamned detective," he said.

"I read a lot on stakeouts," I said. "Let's talk a little about the play."

"Handy Dandy?"

"Yeah. If you talk slowly, I'll be able to follow you."

"I'm not buying that pose," Christopholous said. "You know a lot more than you look like you know."

"Be hard to know less," I said. "What do you think is in this play that stirs up so much opposition."

"Albeit crudely," Christopholous said, "it challenges everyone's preconceptions. Not just the preconceptions of right or left, of racism or humanism, but all. If you come in with compassionate preconceptions about women or blacks, it destroys them. If you come in with hostile preconceptions about women or blacks, it destroys them. It challenges people to consider each human experience directly, without a historic framework."

"A historic framework is not useless," I said.

"Certainly not," Christopholous said. "But Leonard would argue that you must first tear down the jerry-rigged facade, before you can begin to build a sound framework. Leonard O annoys everyone: secular humanists, fundamentalist Christians, conservatives, liberals, libertarians, blacks, whites, women, men, Jews, homosexuals, heterosexuals, bisexuals, Hari Krishnas, the AMA, you name it."

"Leonard's the playwright?" I said.

"Yes."

"Is that O?" I said, "as in '——say can you see?' or as in 'Story of——'?"

"The latter."

"Is it his real name?" I said.

"I doubt it."

"I'll need to talk with him."

"That should be interesting," Christopholous said.

chapter
7

I sat in DeSpain's office in the back corner of the squad room in the neat, square, one-story, red-brick Port City Police Station. DeSpain had his coat off and his gun unholstered and lying on the desk next to the phone.

"Damn thing gets me in the ribs every time I lean back," he said.

"Trouble with the nines," I said. "They're not comfy."

DeSpain shrugged the way a horse does when a fly lands on him.

"You got something on the Sampson killing, or you just in to chew the fat?"

"I was hoping you had something."

"Here's everything I got," DeSpain said. "Killer was probably male. There's no agreement on what he was wearing, except that it was black. Had on some kind of a black mask with eye holes cut into it. He came in during the play and stood at the top of the aisle maybe ten minutes. People figured he was part of the play. The piece might have been a target gun, though to tell you the truth none of the eyewitnesses know a handgun from their pee pee. What everybody agrees is, he fired one shot and put the gun away, and walked out. Nobody saw where he went. ME took a .22 long out."

DeSpain picked up his gun and aimed it over my shoulder.

"Bingo," he said. "Through his heart."

"Maybe the guy's a shooter," I said. "Sort of showing off with the .22."

"There was a fad a while back like that," DeSpain said. "Mob guys were using .22s."

"Or maybe it's the only gun he could get his hands on."

"And it was a lucky shot," DeSpain said.

"What do you know about the victim?"

"What is this, Travelers' fucking Aid?" DeSpain said.

"Hey, I'm telling you all I know," I said.

"You haven't told me shit," DeSpain said.

"True, but it's all I know."

DeSpain shook his head and turned the gun on his desk in a slow circle with his finger through the trigger guard.

"Don't know much more than you do. Studied acting in New York. Was in some plays I never heard of in places I never heard of. Got a job up here. Kept to himself. Stayed out of trouble. Sound like we're closing in?"

"Prints?"

"No record of him ever being fingerprinted."

"So what do you think?" I said.

"I think neither one of us knows shit," DeSpain said. He kept the gun turning slowly.

"Well," I said. "It was about something?"

"Usually is," DeSpain said.

"Yeah, but this more than most," I said. "I mean, if you just want the guy dead you don't dress up in a black costume and shoot him dead on stage in a crowded theater."

"Wouldn't be how I'd do it," DeSpain said.

"That's right. But somebody wanted to make a point."

"And did," DeSpain said. He grinned a big, wolfish grin. "Except we don't know what the point was."

"He was there for a while," I said. "What was he waiting for?"

"Maybe for Sampson to come to the front," DeSpain said. "Get a clear shot."

"Or maybe for Sampson to say the lines he was saying so that the killing would have meaning."

"To whom?"

"I don't know."

"Me either," DeSpain said. He stopped twirling the gun and drummed lightly on it with a forefinger the size of a sap.

"But it might have to do with love," I said. "It's what he was singing about when he got shot."

"Lucky in love," DeSpain said.

"So you've been thinking about it too," I said.

"Some," DeSpain said.

"So maybe it would mean something to a lover," I said.

"'Cept he didn't have one," DeSpain said.

"That you know about," I said.

"You know about one?"

"No."

DeSpain did his wolfish smile again, pulling his lips away from his teeth with no hint of warmth or humor. He had big teeth, with prominent canines.

"Maybe it was a fruitcake," he said. "Thinks he's a Ninja assassin. Buys a ticket. Walks in the front door, puts on his mask, works up his courage, does the deed."

"And that's why he stood there for however many minutes, working up his courage," I said.

"Sure. Ain't so easy for some people."

"You got a whacko file?" I said.

"Sure."

"Anybody fill the bill?"

"Not till we get desperate," DeSpain said.

"Then you make do," I said.

"I've squeezed a lot of square pegs into a lot of round holes," DeSpain said. "Just need to shove sort of hard."

DeSpain had picked up the handgun and was now twirling it by the trigger guard around his forefinger, like a movie cowboy.

"You been a cop," he said.

"Can I see the file?" I said.

Still playing with the handgun DeSpain reached over to the computer on the side table behind his desk and turned it on with his left hand. When the screen brightened, he tapped the keys for a minute. A list of names formed on the screen.

"Want a printout?" he said. "Or you want to read it off the screen?"

"Printout," I said.

DeSpain turned on the printer, hit a couple of keys, and the list began to print.

"Couple years," DeSpain said, "these things'll violate a suspect's civil rights for you. Won't have to lift a finger."

The paper eased out of the printer and DeSpain picked it up and handed it to me. He pointed at the list with the muzzle of the gun.

"Ding dongs are hard to keep track of," he said. "List may need an update."

I nodded.

"You learn anything, you'll dash right on in here and tell me about it," DeSpain said.

"Sure. Who's working the case?"

"Me," DeSpain said.

"Keeping your hand in?" I said.

"Sure."

"I find something, I'll let you know," I said.

"'Preciate it," DeSpain said. He scratched a spot behind his ear with the muzzle of the gun. "We're fighting crime up here day and night," he said. "Day and fucking night."

"Eternal vigilance is the price of liberty," I said.

DeSpain's wolfish grin flashed again. It was almost a reflex. There was no humor in the grin, or in the eyes that were as hard and flat as two stones.

"Yeah," he said. "It is, isn't it."

chapter
8

We were in front of a three-hundred-year-old farmhouse set on twelve acres about three miles from the center of Concord, waiting for the real-estate lady. The house didn't look its age, but it didn't look my age either. The foundation plantings were overgrown, the paint was peeling, some of the windowsills had shriveled and warped. The land rolled gently down toward a stream and merged with thickly forested wetlands, where the deciduous trees were already beginning to turn. From most places on the property you could see no other human sign.

Pearl the Wonder Dog raced around in steadily widening circles, her nose to the ground, her short tail erect. After every full circle she would come to stand in front of Susan with her mouth open, and stare up at her for a moment. Susan would pat her, and Pearl would dash off in another circle.

A single blue jay curved in past some pine trees and settled on the lawn and cocked his head and listened for worms. He heard none and went up again, circling closer to us before he settled on the limb of a red maple. Like most birds he seemed never completely at rest, moving his head, fluttering his wings, making brief, abrupt hops on his tree limb for no reason that I could see. On the other hand, he may have thought me sluggish, leaning against the car in the last glimmer of sunlight beside this striking woman. Probably at least thirteen ways of looking at a blue jay.

"This is the house," Susan said.

"Perfect," I said. "Having established that we cannot live together, we should buy a house in the country together."

"We have also established that we can spend weekends together," Susan said.

"That's because you always distract me with endless sexual invention," I said.

"Doesn't seem endless to me," Susan said. "Ever since I sold the Maine place I've thought we should buy a weekend place out of the city, with some land we could fence, so the baby could run around and point birds."

"Pearl's instincts run more to pointing Oreo cookies, I think."

Susan ignored me.

"And this is the place. It's run down so we can buy it cheap. Then you'll fix it up, and we'll come here with Pearl on autumn weekends and roast chestnuts and have a nice time."

When she was really intense about something she paid very little attention to anything else. Except, usually, me.

"We always have a nice time," I said.

"Yes. We do," Susan said. "Are you making any progress in Port City?"

"Sure. Hawk's watching Christopholous and no one's following him," I said. "I had a nice talk with DeSpain."

"Does he know anything?"

"No. He gave me the psycho list, but there's nothing on it that helps."

"Is he any good?" Susan said.

"DeSpain. Yeah. He's a good cop. Very tough cop."

"Too tough?"

"Some people thought so," I said.

"Tougher than you?"

"Never a horse that couldn't be rode, little lady. Never a rider that couldn't be throwed."

"Good heavens," Susan said. "Does that mean he might be?"

"Means maybe we'll find out some day," I said. "What do you know about Rikki Wu?"

"Rikki?"

"Yeah. It's not much, but so far she's the only one who's objected to my looking into the murder."

"Oh, well, yes, I suppose so. It's hard to take Rikki seriously."

"Somebody does," I said. "If she pawned the jewelry she was wearing the other night, she could buy this house."

"Her husband, Lonnie Wu, is very wealthy, and Rikki is totally indulged. A Chinese American Princess. It has left her with a feeling of near total entitlement."

"Perhaps we should introduce her to Pearl," I said.

"A Canine American Princess," Susan said. "Rikki gives large sums of money to the theater."

"And now she's on the board," I said. "Can you arrange for me to have lunch with her?"

"I'm not sure she'd be willing to see you."

"Mention to her about me being hunk city."

"I'll ask her to lunch with both of us, and then I'll have a crisis with a patient and you can convey my apologies."

"Okay," I said. "But I think hunk city would have worked just as well."

"Rikki's too self-centered to be flirtatious," Susan said.

"Shows what you know," I said.

"You seriously think . . ." Susan started, but Pearl started barking and jumping around, and the real-estate lady pulled up in her maroon Volvo station wagon. When the real-estate lady got out, Pearl dashed up to her and rammed her head between the real-estate lady's thighs.

"How embarrassing," Susan said.

The real-estate lady smiled and patted Pearl. She didn't mind at all. She knew Pearl's owner was a live one.

"House needs a lot of work," I said.

"We prefer the term 'great potential,'" the real-estate lady said.

"I bet you do," I said.

"In this price range. In a lower price range we would prefer the term 'handyman's special,'" she said.

"You like this kind of work," Susan said to me.

"At my own pace," I said.

"Of course," Susan said and smiled at me.

I smiled back. I didn't believe her for a moment, but her smile was worth any servitude. Which is how I found myself, an hour later, the co-owner of a very large house, with a jumbo mortgage, on a street where other home owners raised cows and rode horses and drove Volvo station wagons.

If I weren't so heroic, I would have been nervous.

chapter
9

I felt like a college recruiter. All day I had been sitting in the back row of the empty theater interviewing people about Craig Sampson. I had begun at eight in the morning with Leonard O, himself, in to audition for Craig Sampson's replacement. The first thing I noticed was that Leonard had no beard. It wasn't that he was clean-shaven; he appeared never to have needed a shave. His blond hair was shoulder-length and lank. He had a small voice like the bleat of a goat, and he chewed gum very rapidly. *I trow he were a gelding or a mare.*

We shook hands. His eyes seemed not to register me, and his handshake was a limp squeeze with the tips of his fingers.

"I don't have much time," he said. "I have a full day of listening to actors botch my lines."

He didn't look at me when he spoke. His gaze flitted without apparent purpose.

"I'm looking into Sampson's murder," I said.

"Murder is the bloodiest of the creative arts," he said.

"I kind of figured it was a destructive art," I said.

"The death of the individual may be destructive," O said. "But the act itself, its conception and performance, may be quite artful."

"Encores are hard."

O was scornful.

"Like so many people you conceive of art in the narrowest possible terms," he said. "Museum art."

"I love that Norman Rockwell, don't you?" I said.

"Don't be ridiculous," O said.

"Any reasons you can think of why someone would kill Craig Sampson?" I said.

O's gaze flickered past me. His eyes were never still, and he never looked at me except in passing.

"Of course, dozens of reasons: unrequited love, passion, jealousy, vengeance, lust expressed through violence, political zeal, money, greed . . ."

O shrugged as if to indicate that he had but scratched the surface.

"Pride, lust, envy, anger, covetousness, gluttony, and sloth," I said. "I thought of those too. Anything less general?"

"I knew him only as an actor in my play. He was inadequate. But all the other candidates were even more so."

"What was his greatest failing?" I said.

"Passion. He mouthed the words like a player piano. He did not feel the emotive rhythms that stirred beneath the language."

"I noticed that too," I said.

O's eyes moved rapidly. He chewed his gum.

"It is the greatest frustration of any playwright, that his art emerges only through the instrumentation of actors. Almost by definition the soul that wishes to act is far too narrow to carry the burden of an artist's vision."

"Bummer," I said.

O's glance jittered past me as it moved from one blank wall to another. His eyes were pale blue, and as flat as the bottom of a pie plate.

"Is there anything in the play that I might have missed, that would cause a murder?" I said.

"Almost certainly," O said. "My play speaks to the deepest impulses of humanity, and challenges its most profoundly held beliefs. To the small part of humanity capable of full response, the challenge is very threatening, and a cleansing rage is one possible response."

"In addition to pity and terror," I said.

It almost made O look at me for a minute. But he caught himself and slid his look onto a wall and chewed his gum very swiftly.

"Have you ever been threatened?" I said.

"To be human is to be threatened," O said.

His neck was thin and would wring easily if someone were of a mind.

"Could you tell me about it?" I said.

"The threat of humanity?" O shook his head sadly. "I have been telling you about it for my whole theatrical life."

"Any specific threats from a specific human?"

O shrugged and shook his head as if the question were tedious.

"Have you ever been followed?"

O rocked back a little in mock amazement.

"Excuse me?" he said.

"Followed, stalked, shadowed?"

O almost smiled. "By the angel of death, perhaps."

"Besides him," I said. "Or her."

"What an odd question, why do you ask?"

"I'm an odd guy, have you?"

"Of course not."

We sat for a moment looking at each other. O was working on the gum as if he had only a few more minutes to subdue it.

"I have a question for you, Spenser," he said. "Did you understand anything in my play when you saw it?"

"Actually I did, O—the Tiresias stuff you stole from Eliot."

A startling flush of red blossomed suddenly on O's smooth white face. He stood up.

"I do not steal," he said. "That was homage."

"Of course," I said. "It always is."

chapter
10

Deirdre's chest was no less aggressive than it had been at the reception, and neither was she.

"Alone at last," she said when she sat down.

She might have been twenty-five, with wide blue eyes, and a lot of auburn hair, worn big. Her dark green spandex health club gear was iridescent. An oversized gray sweatshirt reached nearly to her knees. It had a New York Giants logo on the front.

"Craig Sampson's loss is our gain," I said.

"Oh, I'm sorry," she said. "I don't mean to be frivolous about something so awful."

"I doubt that it makes much difference to Sampson," I said. "What can you tell me about him?"

"He was fun," Deirdre said. "He'd been around, you know, and he knew the score."

"Which was what?"

"Excuse me?"

"The score? What was it?"

"Oh, you know what I mean. He was older. He knew the whole downtown theater scene in New York. He'd done cruise ships and dinner theaters. He was good to talk to about the business."

"He ever in any trouble you know of?"

"Craig? No. He was too smart. He kept his nose clean and his mouth shut and went about his business."

"Love life?"

"He wasn't gay. I'm pretty sure. In the theater it's not that big a deal, you know? And besides, I could tell. He was straight."

"Did he have a girlfriend?"

"Nobody in the company. I don't know why. He had plenty of chances, but he didn't seem interested."

"Outside the company?"

Deirdre was sitting sideways on the chair with her legs tucked under her. It was hard to figure how she'd achieved that position, but it made her look good, so I assumed it wasn't accidental.

"Oh, I don't know," she said. "Most of us don't have much life outside the company. You know? I mean Port City . . . really!"

"Did he go away much? Boston? New York?"

"Not that I can remember. Most of us are working most of the time. He'd go to New York a couple times when the theater was dark, make a commercial, he said."

"What commercials?"

"I don't know. I never watch television. And I don't ever want to do commercials. Craig said it covered expenses."

"He have an agent?"

"I don't know."

"Management of any kind?"

"I don't know."

"How'd he get the commercials?"

"I don't know. It wasn't a big deal. He'd go away occasionally and come back and say he'd made a commercial. It's not cool to ask a lot of stuff about things like that."

"Except when I do it," I said.

"Oh, anything you do is cool," Deirdre said.

"It's a gift," I said.

She grinned at me, full of herself, pleased with her body, enjoying her sexiness, glad about her vocation, optimistic about the future, younger than a new Beaujolais.

"So what do you think? You got any clues yet?"

"Not yet."

"Do you get a lot of cases that are hard to figure out?"

"Well, the process sort of selects them out. People don't usually call me if the local cops solve it promptly. Even then, though, most cases aren't complicated to solve. A lot of them are more complicated to resolve."

"What do you mean?"

"I mean sometimes I know who did what, but I'm not sure what I should do about it."

"What do you do?" Deirdre said.

"I normally have two courses of action. I follow my best instincts guided by experience, or I do what Susan says."

Deirdre grinned again.

"I bet you don't do what anyone says."

Without moving, she appeared somehow wiggly.

"Do you ever get a case where there are no clues? You know, when you can, like, never figure out who did it."

"I solve all my cases," I said. "Some of them are just not solved yet."

Deirdre clapped quietly.

"Great line," she said.

"Thanks, I'm trying it out for my ad in the Yellow Pages."

chapter
11

Wearing a spiffy white raincoat beaded with rain drops, and carrying a wet umbrella that looked like a Chinese parasol, Rikki Wu came into her husband's restaurant as if she were walking onto a yacht. The guy at the register jumped up and took her coat and umbrella and disappeared with them. No one had paid any attention to my coat, which I had hung on the back of a chair. She scanned the room looking for Susan. The place was nearly empty for lunch. Maybe it was the rain. Or maybe most people in downtown Port City didn't do lunch. Her eyes swept past me, and stopped, and came back and stayed.

I stood. She walked over to me.

"Mrs. Wu," I said.

"Where's Susan?"

"She had an emergency with a patient," I said.

I held Rikki Wu's chair for her. She seemed puzzled.
"So it's just the two of us?" she said.

"Yes, but I'll be twice as lively and amusing to make up," I said.

Rikki Wu looked uneasy, but she sat.

The restaurant had begun, in another time, before it was a pizzeria, as a store with glass windows facing the street. The windows were half curtained in some sort of accordion-pleated white paper. Above the curtains, the glass was fogged by the wet weather. A waiter brought us tea, and stood quietly beside us. He was as close to prostrating himself as he could get while standing. Without looking at him, Rikki Wu spoke in rapid Chinese. He bowed and backed away and disappeared.

"I hope you don't mind," Rikki Wu said in a voice that sounded like she didn't care if I minded or not. "I took the liberty of ordering for us."

"I don't mind," I said.

I watched her accept the fact that she was alone with me, and watched as her persona adjusted to the fact. She smiled at me. There was a touch of conspiratorial intimacy in the smile. Rikki Wu was sex. I was pretty sure she was spoiled and self-centered and shallow. Maybe cruel. Certainly careless about other people. But she was sex. She would like sex, she would need it, she would want more of it than most people were prepared to give her, and she would be totally self-absorbed during it. I'd spent too many years looking for it, and occasionally at it, not to know it when I saw it. And I was seeing it. She would be a hell of a good time once a month.

"Well," she said, "here we are."

"Sleepy-eyed and yawning," I said. "See how late it gets."

"You're sleepy?"

"It's a song lyric. I have these momentary flights now and then."

"Oh, how interesting."

The waiter arrived, placed a large platter of assorted dim sum before us, and bowed himself away. Rikki Wu put several items on my plate.

"Thank you," I said. "Did you know Craig Sampson very well?"

"Oh, no."

"You seemed very protective of him the other night."

"I admired him, his work," Rikki Wu said. "He was a fine actor. And I did not like the innuendo of your questions."

Her English was perfect, and formal-sounding. Her Chinese had sounded fluent too, though I had no way to judge that, except that it had been rapid.

"Yeah. I'm sorry I had to ask. Were you born here?"

"In Port City?"

"In the United States."

"No. In T'ai-pei."

"So your English is acquired."

She smiled.

"Yes. It's interesting that you should notice."

"It sounds like your native language," I said.

"Yes. It is. So is Cantonese, which I just spoke to the waiter. And Mandarin."

"You speak the Chinese dialects as well as you speak English?"

"Oh, certainly."

"What do you think in?" I said.

"Excuse me?"

"When you're alone, thinking about things, what language do you think in?"

She hesitated, and drank some tea. Maybe she never thought about anything when she was alone.

"I don't know . . . I guess it depends what I'm thinking about." She smiled. "Or who."

"Do you think much about Craig Sampson?"

"Yes, it's so tragic. Such a brilliant young man, his life cut short so suddenly."

"Did you think about him much before he died."

Her eyes widened. She sipped some more tea. Then her eyes narrowed a little and she looked sternly at me over the tea cup.

"What are you trying to imply?" she said coldly.

"Mrs. Wu, I'm just talking. I'm just looking for a handhold. I mean no innuendo."

"There was nothing between Craig and me. I barely knew him off stage."

"You live here in Port City?"

"On the hill," she said.

"Of course. Did he have any relationship with any of the women in town that you know of?"

"Why did he have to have a relationship? I know of no relationships he had in town or anywhere else. Why do you keep asking that?"

"Because most people have one, even if only of a fleeting sexual nature. And he seems to have had none. That's maybe a little unusual. If you don't know anything, you pay attention to the *unusual.*"

"Well, why do you keep asking me?"

"I keep asking everyone. You're just the one that's here."

"Well, I find it very boring," Rikki Wu said.

"Okay. We'll turn our attention to more exciting stuff," I said. "Would you like to see me do a one-armed pushup?"

"Can you really do that?" she said.

"As many as you'd like."

She relaxed. We were back in the realm of the physical. This was her turf.

"You must be very strong," she said.

"But pure," I said. "And kind-hearted."

"Perhaps you will show me sometime, when we are not in so public a place."

"I could meet you at the gym," I said.

She frowned. Maybe I wasn't as funny as I thought I was. Or maybe she didn't have much sense of humor. Probably a Chinese thing. I ate some dim sum. She drank some tea. The dim sum wasn't very good. But there was plenty of it.

"Do you work out?" she said.

"Sure," I said.

"I do too. Do you have a trainer?"

"No, I muddle through on my own."

"I have two," she said. "My CV specialist, and Ronny, my strength and conditioning coach."

"CV?"

"Cardiovascular," she said. "I train with them every day."

"Well, it seems to be working," I said.

"Yes. You should see my body," she said.

"Yes, I should."

She laughed. It wasn't an embarrassed laugh. But it was an uneasy one, as if she feared her own sexuality and where it might lead her. She stood. For lunch she had consumed two cups of green tea. I stood.

"I have to go to my body-sculpting class," she said. "Sometime you must show me that pushup."

"One arm," I said. "Ask Ronny if he can do that."

She laughed. I gave her my card.

"You think of anything useful, call me," I said.

"Perhaps I will," she said.

The waiter appeared with her coat and held it while she put it on.

"Lunch is taken care of," she said.

She turned and walked to the door. The waiter followed her, and when she got to the door, he opened it, and popped her umbrella open and held it over her head until she took the handle from him and walked out. I'm not sure she ever saw the waiter.

chapter
12

It was a bright day in Concord. The sky above the old house was the kind of bright blue that you see in seventeenth-century Dutch paintings. The sun was strong and pleasant and the foliage was turning color.

The grounds around the house seemed to have been landscaped by Tarzan of the apes. Bushes, vines, saplings, weeds, decorative plantings run amok, all looped and sagged around the house, clustered in front of it, clung to it, and concealed far too much of it.

"This is ugly," Susan said. She had on jeans, and sneakers, and a lavender tee shirt with the sleeves cut off. Sweat had darkened the tee shirt. Sweat ran down her face under the long billed Postrio baseball cap. A sheen of sweat defined the small, hard muscles in her forearms.

"They'd never recognize you at Bergdorf's," I said.

She paid no attention, focusing as she always did on

the question before her. She was wearing tan leather work gloves and carrying an axe.

"We need a chain saw," Susan said.

"Jesus," I said.

"You don't think I can handle a chain saw?"

"They're sort of dangerous," I said. "If I weren't totally fearless, I'd be a little afraid of chain saws."

"Well, it would speed things up," she said.

"What's the hurry? We have the rest of our life to do this."

"You know perfectly well that I am always in a hurry."

"Almost always," I said.

"Except then."

Pearl came galloping up the slope from the stream, and jumped up with both feet on Susan's chest. Susan leaned forward so that Pearl could lap her face, which Pearl did vigorously. Susan squinched and endured the lapping until Pearl spotted a squirrel and dropped down and stalked it.

"God, wasn't that awful," Susan said.

"You might tell her not to do that," I said.

"She likes to do that," Susan said.

The squirrel zipped up a tree, and when it was safely out of reach, Pearl dashed at it and jumped up with her forepaws against the tree gazing after it.

"You think she'd actually eat the squirrel?" Susan said.

"She eats everything else she finds," I said.

Susan took a big swing with her axe at the base of a tree-sized shrub. What she lacked in technique, she made up in vigor, and I decided not to mention that she swung like a girl. I went back inside and worked on demolishing the back stairs with a three-pound sledge and a crowbar.

I had a radio playing jazz in the kitchen. Pearl moseyed around in the fenced-in fields finding disgusting things to roll in. She came back periodically to show off her new smell, negotiating the debris with easy dignity. I could see Susan through the front windows. She had her axe, her long-handled clippers, her bow saw, and her machete. She hacked and cut and clipped and sawed and stopped periodically to haul the cuttings into a big pile for pickup. Her tee shirt was dark with sweat. But, she was, I knew, tireless. For all of her self-mocking parody of the Jewish American Princess, she loved to work. And was rarely more happy than when she was fully engaged.

I got the crowbar under one edge of the lath and plaster wall and pried away a big chunk, exposing one of the stair stringers. With the three-pound sledge I knocked the stringer loose and the stairs canted slowly and then came down with a satisfying crash.

This is a lot better, I thought, *than trying to find who killed Craig Sampson.*

chapter
13

I was in my office with my feet up, drinking coffee from a paper cup and reading "Doonesbury." Behind me, two stories down, on Berkeley Street, tourists, brightly lit by the October sun, were posing with the teddy bear sculpture outside F. A. O. Schwarz. I finished "Doonesbury" and watched the photography for a moment, speculating on the tendency of tourists to be larger than their wardrobes. I was able to reach no conclusion about that, so I gave up and turned to the sports page to read "Tank McNamara." I was rereading it to make sure I'd missed no hidden meaning when my door opened and in came three Asian guys. The door opened straight onto the corridor. I had no waiting room. I'd had one once in another location and no one had ever waited in it. One Private Eye. No Waiting. I folded the paper and put it down on the desk and said hello.

The tallest one did the talking.

"You're Mister Spenser?" he said.

"Yeah."

"My name is Lonnie Wu," he said. "I believe you know my wife."

"Rikki," I said.

"Yes."

Lonnie Wu was maybe 5′ 10″ and slim. He had polished black hair combed straight back, and a small, neat black moustache. He was wearing a gray cashmere jacket with a big red picture frame plaid in it that fitted him as if they had grown up together, and probably cost more than my whole wardrobe. He wore a black silk shirt buttoned to the neck, and black slacks, and black loafers that were shinier than his hair.

"Have a seat," I said.

He coiled fluently into my client chair. There was only one. He said something to the two guys who'd come with him, and they stood against the wall on either side of my office door. I opened the right-hand top drawer of my desk a little.

"Couple of waiters from the restaurant?" I said.

"No."

"They from the north?"

"They are from Vietnam."

Wu smiled. The companions seemed to be barely out of their teens. They were both shorter than Wu, small-boned and lank-haired. One of them had a horizontal scar maybe two inches long under his left eye. They both wore jeans and sneakers and maroon satin jackets. The guy without the scar wore a blue bandana on his head.

"You are a detective," Wu said.

I nodded.

"And you are investigating the murder of an actor in Port City."

I nodded again.

"You had lunch recently with my wife."

"Sure," I said. "In your restaurant."

"And you questioned her."

"I question everybody," I said. "While you're here, I'll probably question you."

"I wish to know why you are questioning my wife."

"See previous answer," I said.

"Excuse me?"

"Like I said, I question everybody. Your wife is simply one of the people involved with the theater."

"My wife," Wu said calmly, "is not 'simply' anything. She is Mrs. Lonnie Wu. And I would prefer that you not speak to her again."

"How come?" I said.

"It is unseemly."

"Mrs. Wu didn't seem to think so," I said.

"What Mrs. Wu thinks is not of consequence. It is unseemly for her to be having lunch with a *low faan.*"

"Is *low faan* a term of racial endearment?"

"It is an abbreviated form of *guey low faan,* which means barbarian," Wu said. "Though many people use it merely to indicate someone who is not Chinese."

I nodded.

"You don't fully subscribe, then, to the melting pot theory," I said.

"Nor do I wish to stand here and make small talk," Wu said. "I think it would be best if you stayed out of Port City."

"Is it okay if I retain my U.S. citizenship?" I said.

"What you do outside of Port City is your business. But if you come back . . ." he moved his head in such a way as to include the two Vietnamese kids against the wall . . . "we will make it our business."

The kids were silent. As far as I could tell, they understood nothing of what was being said. But they didn't seem to care. They seemed relaxed against the wall. Their dark eyes were empty of everything but energy.

"So that's what the teeny boppers are for," I said.

"I don't know teeny bopper," Wu said.

"Adolescents," I said.

Wu nodded. I could see him file the phrase away. He'd know it next time.

"Don't be misled," Wu said. "They are boat people. They are older than their age."

"And empty," I said.

Wu smiled.

"Entirely," he said. "They will do whatever I tell them to."

I looked at the kids for a moment. They were not something new. They were something very old, without family, or culture; prehistoric, deracinated, vicious, with no more sense of another's pain than a snake would have when it swallowed a rat. I'd seen atavistic kids like this before: homegrown black kids so brutalized by life that they had no feelings except anger. It was what made them so hard. They weren't even bad. Good and bad were meaningless to them. Everything had been taken from them. They had only rage. And it was the rage that sustained them, that animated their black eyes, and energized the slender, empty place intended for their souls. The kids saw me looking at them and looked back at me without discomfort, without, in fact, anything at all. I looked back at Wu. He had crossed his legs and was lighting a cigarette.

"We got a problem here, Mr. Wu."

"You have a problem," Wu said.

I shrugged.

"Let me tell you my problem," I said. "I am a sort of professional tough guy. I'm kind of smart, and I've got a lot of experience. But mainly I get hired to do things other people can't do, or won't do, or don't dare do. You know?"

Wu inhaled, enjoyed it, and let it out slowly, through his nose. He didn't say anything.

"So," I said, "how would it look if I let two juvenile delinquents and a Chinese guy half my size come in here and frighten me."

"It would not look good," Wu said. "But you would be alive."

My hand was resting on my desk top just above the half-open drawer.

"All this because I had lunch with your wife."

"You will stay away from Port City," Wu said. "Or you will be killed."

I dropped my hand to the open drawer and came out with a revolver, which I cocked as I took it out. At the first movement both the Vietnamese kids went under their coats, but I had about a two-second lead on them and was aimed at the tip of Wu's nose by the time they got their guns out. Both had nines.

"If I hear the hammer go back on either of those guns," I said to Wu, "you're dead."

Wu spoke to the boys. Peripherally I could see both kids crouching, holding the gun in both hands.

"Perhaps they are already cocked," Wu said.

He hadn't moved, nor had his expression changed.

"Then I'm dead," I said.

The office was silent. I listened. Even these kids

weren't crazy enough to walk around with a round in the chamber and the hammer back. It was a good bet. But it was still a bet. There was no sound. I'd won the bet.

"Even if you do shoot me," Wu said, "they'll kill you."

"I'm pretty good," I said. "Maybe they won't."

My gun was a Smith and Wesson .357. Six rounds. It had a blued finish and a walnut grip, and it was alleged to stop a charging bear. Normally, unless I expected to encounter a bear, I carried a comfy little .38. But for office use the .357 was an effective negotiating tool. I kept my eyes on Wu. I was listening so hard I felt tired. The radiator pinged in the corner and almost cost Wu his life. Still he didn't move. Still the kids crouched. Still I held steady on the end of his nose. Then Wu said something to the Vietnamese kids. Both of them put their guns away. I leaned back a little in my chair and kept the gun on Wu.

"Tell them to put the guns on the floor," I said.

Wu spoke to the boys. They answered.

"You will have to kill them, if you can, to get their guns away," Wu said.

The boys stared straight at me with their empty eyes. I was wrong. They had more than rage. They had face, and they wouldn't give it up. And I couldn't make them. I knew that. I could kill them. But I couldn't make them lose face.

"Maybe another time," I said. "See you around."

Wu looked at me for another moment. Then without a word he dropped his burning cigarette on the floor and got up and left. Without even glancing at me, the two kids went after him. They didn't look back. They didn't close the door.

I sat with my chair tilted back and the gun still in my hand. A thin blue will-o'-the-wisp trailed up from the still-burning cigarette. I stared through it, out the door, at the empty corridor. After a while I got up and went around and stepped on the cigarette. I closed the door and went back to my desk and got the phone, and called Boston Police Headquarters. I asked for Homicide. When I got Homicide I asked for Lt. Quirk. He picked up his phone, still talking to someone, and held it while he finished the conversation.

"Fuck ATF," he said to someone. "They got their problems. We got ours."

Then he spoke into the phone.

"Quirk."

"Hi," I said. "This is the ATF charitable fund . . ."

"I know who it is. What do you want?"

"You got a Chinatown guy?"

"Yeah."

"I need to talk with him."

"Okay. Name's Herman Leong. I'll have him call you."

"Thanks," I said. But Quirk had already hung up.

Mister Congenial.

chapter
14

At ten in the morning, Hawk and I were drinking coffee at a too-small table, in front of a rain-streaked window, in a joint called the Happy Haddock Coffee Shop on Ocean Street near the theater. Handmade signs behind the counter advertised linguiça with eggs, kale soup, and pork stew with clams.

"Think we should have some kale soup?" Hawk said.

"No," I said. "Couple of all-natural donuts."

"Good choice," Hawk said.

He got up and went to the counter and returned with four plain donuts on a plate.

"Authentic crime-buster food," Hawk said.

The Happy Haddock was almost empty. There was a dark-haired kid on the counter with a ponytail and an insufficient moustache. He wore a stained apron and a pink tee shirt with *Pixies World Tour* printed on the front.

An old woman in a shapeless dress and a bandana was scraping the grill with an inverted spatula. A couple of old men in plaid shirts and plastic baseball caps sat at the counter drinking coffee and smoking.

"Nobody shadowing the Greek," Hawk said. "'Cept me."

"If there ever was," I said.

"You think he made it up?"

"No."

"You think he thought he was being followed and he wasn't?"

"No."

"You confused, don't know what to think?"

"Yeah."

Hawk nodded.

"Maybe there never was a shadow," he said. "Or maybe the shadow laying low 'cause the murder stirred everybody up. Or maybe the shadow got wind of me. What I know is, if there was a shadow, he didn't spot me."

"I know."

"I'm getting bored," Hawk said.

"Yeah," I said. "Forget it. There may be a shadow, but not while you're around."

Hawk broke off a smallish piece of his second donut and ate it and wiped his fingers carefully on the paper napkin.

"You got anything?" he said.

"Yeah," I said. "But I don't know what it is."

Hawk ate another piece of donut and waited.

"Woman named Rikki Wu is on the theater board with Susan. I had lunch with her couple days ago to talk about the murder."

"She Chinese?"

"Yes."

"Good-looking?"

"Yes."

"I like Chinese women," Hawk said.

"Also Irish women, Aleut women, French women, women from Katmandu . . ."

"Never bopped nobody from Katmandu," Hawk said.

"Their loss," I said. "Anyway. She didn't do me much good, but the next day her husband, Lonnie Wu, came to my office with two teen-aged Vietnamese gunnies, and told me to buzz off."

"How nice," Hawk said in his BBC voice. "He's mastered the American idiom."

"Told me to stay away from his wife."

"Who wouldn't?" Hawk said.

"Told me to stay out of Port City, too."

"Awful worried 'bout his wife," Hawk said.

"Or something," I said.

"Or something," Hawk said. "He say what he gonna do if you don't stay away?"

"I believe he mentioned killing me."

"Un huh," Hawk said. "If he do, can I have your donut?"

"Yeah, but you got to finish that house in Concord for Susan."

"Sure." Hawk drank some coffee. "Tongs use Vietnamese kids for muscle. Kids don't give a shit. Kill anything."

"Tongs?" I said. "In Port City?"

Hawk shrugged.

"Big Chinatown," he said. "Bigger than Boston."

"True," I said.

"You think it's a tong thing?" Hawk said.

"I don't know."

"You think Wu's involved in the killing?"

"I don't know."

"You saying that a lot."

"Yeah. I'm thinking of having it printed on my business card."

The rain was slower than it had been last time I was in Port City, but it was steady and it made the fall morning dark. The light from the restaurant window reflected on the wet pavement. A Port City police car cruised slowly past, its headlights on, its wipers going. The door of the Happy Haddock opened, bringing with it the rain-dampened smell off the harbor, and Jocelyn Colby came in wearing a belted tan raincoat and carrying a green-and-white umbrella. She closed the umbrella and put it against the wall and walked to our table.

"Thank God," she said. "I saw you through the window. I need to talk."

I gestured at the empty chair. She looked uneasily at Hawk and sat. I introduced them.

"Coffee," I said.

"No. Yes. Black. Thank you."

I got up and got us three cups and brought it back. One of the old men at the counter poked the other one and they both stared at Jocelyn. The kid behind the counter went back to reading *The Want Advertiser*. Probably looking for a deal on moustache wax.

"What's new," I said when I sat down.

Jocelyn looked sideways at Hawk.

"May I speak freely?" she said.

"Sure."

"I . . . it's about the case."

I nodded. She hesitated.

"You can talk in front of Hawk," I said. "He's too dumb to remember what you said."

"Lucky thing too," Hawk said, "cause I a bad blabbermouth."

Jocelyn couldn't tell if she were being kidded. Her glance shifted back and forth.

"Hawk's with me," I said. "You can talk to us."

Jocelyn held her coffee mug in both hands, took a swallow, held the mug against her lower lip, and looked at me over the rim.

"I'm being followed," she said.

Jocelyn waited, allowing the impact of her statement to achieve all it was going to.

"Lot of that going around," Hawk said.

"Tell me about it," I said.

"He's medium height and slender," Jocelyn said. "Black coat and a black slouch hat pulled low."

"When did he start shadowing you?" I said.

"Two nights ago."

"And why not go to the cops?"

"Well . . . I mean, Jimmy said you were here because someone was stalking someone. And then I was hurrying along the street and I saw you . . ."

"Sure," I said. "And I have such a kind face."

"Yes," she said. "You do."

"So what would you like?" I said.

"Like? I . . . Well, I guess I thought you'd want to look into it. I don't know exactly, but . . . in truth, I guess I thought you might want to, ah, protect me."

"Are you saying you want to hire me?"

"Hire?"

"Yeah. I do this for a living. Or I used to, before I came down here."

"Well . . . of course, I . . . I don't have any money."

"Lot of that going around too," Hawk said.

He was looking out at the street. Suddenly he put out

chapter
15

A close-up company was power-screwing plywood panels over the shattered window. The crime scene people were through digging slugs out of the woodwork and had departed. Everyone else had made a statement and gone home, except the old lady who was in the back room making phone calls. DeSpain sat on one of the stools, his elbows resting on the counter behind him.

"So what were you two guys doing up here?"

"Drinking coffee," I said. "Eating donuts."

"Just like real coppers," DeSpain said. "You still working on the murder?"

"Yeah."

"What's Hawk doing here?"

"Helping," Hawk said.

"Helping what?"

"Helping the investigation."

"Hawk." DeSpain looked tired. "You don't fucking investigate."

Hawk smiled.

"What you talking to the broad about?" DeSpain said.

"The murder. I'm trying to talk with everybody about the murder."

"Counter kid says she came in after you."

"Sure," I said. "She knew I wanted to talk with her, saw us here, came in."

DeSpain nodded.

"And Hawk was here in case she got outta hand. Who you figure fired thirty rounds or so through the window at you?"

"What makes it us?" I said.

"Who else was sitting in the window. You hadn't hit the deck, you'd have been dead."

"And nobody else with a scratch," I said.

DeSpain grinned.

"And they didn't hit the deck," he said.

"Sort of suggestive?" I said.

"So," DeSpain said, "say they were after you. Who might they have been?"

I spread my hands.

"Everyone loves us," I said.

DeSpain looked around the room, the back wall pocked with bullet holes, the window nearly boarded up.

"Some more than others," he said.

"Ain't that always the way," I said.

"You got anything to say," DeSpain said to Hawk.

Hawk smiled his friendly smile.

"No," he said.

We all sat. The last piece of plywood went in. The place was quiet.

"Who you got in Port City," I said, "might do this?"

"It's a funny city," DeSpain said. "Population about

125,000. You got about 20,000 WASPs live up on the hill, worry about new Beaujolais and civil rights in The Horn of Africa. Along the waterfront you got some 20,000 Portagies, worry about George's Bank and fava beans. In between, at the bottom of the hill, on the flats inland, you got about 60,000 Chinamen. Sort of a Chink sandwich, between the Yankees and the Portagies. Chinks are worried mostly about staying alive."

"How come so many Chinese?" I said.

"When the mills were here it was mostly French Canuck labor. When the mills pulled out, the Canucks left. The Yankees kept looking for a place to put money. The Portagies kept fishing. They needed fish-processing plants, and they needed cheap labor to make it work."

"Where there's a will, there's a way," I said. "You got any thoughts on who did the shooting?"

"Probably not the Yankees," DeSpain said. "They're not against it, but they'd hire it done."

"Who would they hire?" I said.

DeSpain looked at me and his lips curled back in what he probably thought was a smile.

"Didn't we get confused here?" he said. "I think I'm supposed to ask you questions."

"Just trying to be helpful," I said.

"Yeah," DeSpain said. "Both of you. I'm lucky I don't have to go it alone."

Hawk and I both smiled politely.

"Well, unfortunately, I guess you'll be around," DeSpain said. "I might want to talk with you some more."

"Anytime," I said.

We were all silent again.

"You too, Hawk," DeSpain said after a moment.

"Anytime," Hawk said.

The old lady came out of the back.

"You wanna lock up now, Evangelista?" DeSpain said.

She shook her head.

"Insurance man coming," she said.

"Okay," DeSpain said.

He stood up, a big, solid, healthy-looking guy, with a big friendly face. And eyes like blue basalt.

"Anything comes to mind," he said, "you'll call."

"In a heartbeat," I said.

DeSpain looked at Hawk, opened his mouth, and closed it. He shook his head.

"Of course not," he said and went on out the door. Hawk and I went out after him. DeSpain got in a waiting car and drove away. Hawk and I walked to my car parked by the theater.

"You didn't say nothing about Mr. and Mrs. Wu," Hawk said.

"I know," I said. "DeSpain bothers me."

"Always had the reputation he cut it kind of fine," Hawk said.

"Yeah."

The rain dripped off the bill of my Chicago White Sox cap. I brushed it away. The smell of the rain mixed with the salt smell of the harbor, freshening it, making Port City downtown seem cleaner than it was.

"DeSpain told me the FBI couldn't match Sampson's prints."

"The guy got shot."

"Yeah. But Susan told me he'd gone to school on the GI Bill. Which would mean he was a veteran."

"Which would mean they'd have his prints in Washington."

"Maybe Susan's wrong," Hawk said.

"Maybe."

"Maybe Sampson lied to her."

"Maybe."

Hawk grinned.

"Or maybe DeSpain lying to you."

"Maybe," I said. "I figure I'll just keep still until I find out what the sides are up here."

"Never got in no trouble keeping still," Hawk said.

A nine-passenger van rolled by, its headlights on, its wipers working, splashing water from the gutter onto the sidewalk. In the van were nine Chinese men, waiters probably, going to work.

"Me either."

Hawk was wearing something that looked like a black silk raincoat. The rain beaded up on it in translucent drops before it serpentined down the fabric. He wore no hat, and if he minded the rain on his skull, he didn't show it. On the other hand, except for amusement and not amusement, he never showed anything.

"What we going to do about the lovely Jocelyn?"

"You think she's being followed?"

"No."

"I don't either," I said. "Why don't we believe her?"

"Instinct, babe. We been doing this kind of thing a long time."

"What if we're wrong."

"I'm not usually wrong."

"That's because you're closer to the jungle than I am. But maybe we better be sure."

Hawk shrugged.

"You want me to shadow her?"

"For a while."

"I bet I be the only one," Hawk said.

I shrugged.

"Besides," Hawk said. "They never had no jungles in Ireland. Your ancestors just paint themselves blue and run around in the peat bogs."

"Well, it was a damned nice blue," I said.

chapter
16

A cop I knew named Lee Farrell was working with me in Concord, and when we got the back stairwell down, and the rubble cleaned away, we noticed that the beams supporting the open perimeter of the now stairless well rested, at either end, on nothing at all. As far as we could tell, they were held up by the floor they were supposed to be supporting. This seemed to me an unsound architectural device, so Lee and I went down to Concord Lumber and bought a couple of ten-foot two-by-eights that were long enough to reach the cross members, and scabbed them onto the unsupported beams with ten-penny nails. Then I climbed down off the step ladder and we went out to have lunch with Susan on a picnic table she'd bought and had delivered, under one of the trees she'd pruned. It was October and bright blue, with a background of leaf color, and no wind. There were enough leaves underfoot to help with the autumnal feeling, but the weather was warm, and the sky was cloudless.

"Before you sit down," Susan said, "get me that blue tablecloth out of the car."

I got the tablecloth and started to spread it on the picnic table, and Susan thought that I was not doing a good job and took it over. She got the cloth situated on, and put a purple glass vase with wild flowers in it at one end of the table.

"Isn't that pretty?" Susan said. "Lee found it in one of those closets you ripped out in the dining room."

"Who picked the flowers?" I said.

"Lee," Susan said. "There's a whole sea of them down there." She nodded toward the stream at the foot of the property, where the woods began.

I looked at Farrell. He shrugged.

"I'm gay," he said. "Whaddya want?"

"What next," I said. "A lavender gun?"

Susan put a large takeout bag on the table and began to distribute food.

"Turkey, lettuce, tomato with sweet mustard on fresh whole wheat bread," she said. "There's a nice little sandwich shop in town. And some bread and butter pickles, and some spring water. Does anyone want beer? Or some wine?"

"Rip-out guys don't do wine," I said.

Farrell grinned.

"Whoops," he said.

I settled for spring water, hoping not to sever a limb with the Sawzall, and Lee did the same. Susan had a Diet Coke, warm. Farrell stared at it.

"Diet Coke? Warm?"

"I hate cold things," Susan said.

"People clean battery terminals with warm Diet Coke," Farrell said.

"That's their privilege," Susan said and drank some.

"You working on that thing up in Port City?" Lee said.

"Yes."

Pearl the Wonder Dog came loping up through the stand of wild flowers, jumped effortlessly up onto the table, poked her nose into the takeout bag, and held the point, her tail wagging like the vibrations of a tuning fork.

"She appears to have bayed the sandwiches," Farrell said.

"Get down," Susan said forcefully, and Pearl turned and lapped her face vigorously. I reached across and picked her up and put her on the ground and gave her half my sandwich.

"Isn't that rewarding inappropriate behavior?" Farrell said.

"Yes," I said and gave her the other half of my sandwich and rummaged in the bag for a new one.

Farrell turned and gazed at the house.

"This is a hell of a project," he said.

"Also long-range," I said.

"You going to move in together when it's done."

Susan and I said "No" simultaneously.

Farrell grinned.

"Okay, we're clear on that. You got a plan?"

Susan looked at me. I shrugged.

"Outside," Susan said. "My plan is to cut almost everything down and start over."

"Inside," I said, "I plan to rip nearly everything out and start over."

"But no vision of what it will look like when it's done?"

"Step at a time," I said. "Part of stripping it down is learning about it. You get to know the house, and when it's stripped back to the essentials, it will sort of tell you what to do next."

"Like an investigation," Farrell said.

"Very much like that," I said. "Except the house doesn't lie to you."

"Are they lying to you up in Port City?" Susan said.

"Yeah. Did you tell me that Sampson went to school on the GI Bill?"

"Yes."

"So he was in the military?"

"Yes."

"He told you that?"

"Yes, and showed me pictures of himself, in uniform, in front of some kind of bunkery thing. Why?"

"DeSpain says the FBI has no record of his prints."

"But if he was in the army . . ." Susan said.

"Yeah. They should have them."

"I should be able to run that down for you," Farrell said. "Take a while."

"I'd appreciate it," I said.

Farrell nodded. Pearl had moved under the picnic table and was resting her head on Farrell's leg. He looked down at her and broke off a small portion of his sandwich and fed it to her.

"What do you do about people who don't like having your dog in their lap when they come to visit?" Farrell said.

"We assume there is something wrong with them," Susan said. "And we try to help them."

chapter
17

I met Herman Leong in a diner on South Street. He was a short guy with horn-rimmed glasses, a thick neck, and a close crewcut. His eyes were humorous. He wore a buttoned-up tan sweater under a black suit. When I joined him at the counter, he was eating pancakes. I ordered coffee.

"Quirk says you looking for information about China-town," he said to me.

I stirred some sugar into my coffee. The mug was thick white china veined with spidery cracks.

"Sort of," I said. "You know anything about Port City?"

"Sure."

"I'm into something up there that I don't understand."

"You must be used to that," Herman said.

"Quirk's been bragging about me again," I said. "There's a big Chinese community in Port City."

"Chinatown North."

"Who runs it?"

"Lonnie Wu," Leong said.

"Just like that?" I said.

"Sure. Lonnie Wu is the Port City *dai low* for the Kwan Chang tong."

"What's a *dai low?*"

"Means elder brother," Leong said. "A *dai low* is a gang coordinator. Tongs don't have soldiers any more. It's cheaper and safer and more efficient to sub it out. Mostly now they use street gangs for muscle. The *dai low* recruits kids, organizes them, serves as liaison between them and the tong."

"Wu had a couple of Vietnamese kids with him last time I saw him," I said.

"Probably Death Dragons," Leong said. "That's the Port City gang they use. They're Vietnamese of Chinese descent. Refugees, some of them second generation. You can't deport them. They don't care if they live or die. Don't care if you do. They'll take a contract on a three-month-old baby."

"Does Boston run Port City?"

"The Kwan Chang tong, yeah, through Lonnie Wu. The thing about a *dai low* is that, normally, he's the only tong guy the gang bangers see. They get busted, he bails them out. They go to court, he gets them a lawyer. He pays them. He puts out the contract. So Lonnie's all the Death Dragons know."

"He a big man in the Boston tong?"

"Not exactly. Chinatown is Chinatown. There isn't much that's yes or no, you understand? He's a *dai low*. Theoretically, he's got one contact in Kwan Chang tong.

And, theoretically, I don't know who it is. Nobody's supposed to. *Dai low*s guard that pretty close. That way he's sort of separated from Kwan Chang by the secrecy thing. If only two people connect the tong and the gang, it's hard for the cops to connect them."

Leong finished his pancakes, swirling the last bite around in the syrup on the plate before he put it in his mouth. He chewed it carefully.

"And if only two people know, and the cops find out," I said, "the tong knows who told."

Leong nodded, swallowed his pancake, and drank some coffee. He patted his mouth with a napkin, and took out some cigarettes.

"You mind?" he said.

I shook my head.

"So . . ." Leong put a cigarette in his mouth and rolled it into the corner. He got a Zippo lighter out and snapped a flame and lit the cigarette and put the lighter away with one of those efficient little movements smokers have developed over the long ritual of their addiction. I admired the movement. I kind of missed it, although it had been nearly thirty years since I smoked. He exhaled some smoke.

". . . Lonnie is important to Kwan Chang, but the job means he needs to be kept pretty separate from the tong. Except for one thing. He married in to the family of the guy runs Kwan Chang."

Leong was smoking a Lucky Strike. No filter. The burning tobacco smelled good, although I knew it wasn't.

"So that's why the separation is theoretical," I said. "Who's his in-law?"

"Uncle Eddie Lee. Fast Eddie, Counselor for Life. Lonnie Wu married his sister."

"Doesn't that make it a little complicated?" I said.

"Yeah. Most tong bosses don't want a *dai low* for a brother-in-law. But there it is. And you know how us Chinese are with the family thing. Eddie's the senior male in the family. He's responsible for everyone else, including his brother-in-law. What's your interest?"

"I went up there to look into a murder at the Rep theater. I talked with a bunch of witnesses, the damn killing took place on stage . . ."

Leong nodded.

"I heard about that," he said.

"And one of them was Rikki Wu. Afterwards, her husband came to my office with two shooters and told me to stay away from his wife, and to stay out of Port City. I did stay away from his wife. I didn't stay away from Port City, and a couple days ago somebody drove by and tried to shoot me through the window of a restaurant."

"You're as good as I heard," Leong said. "Death Dragons want you dead, normally you're dead right away."

"I'm an elusive devil," I said.

Leong looked at me with eyes that had seen everything. Nothing impressed him, nothing shocked him, nothing excited him. And it was not just what he had seen; his eyes held the history of a people who for millennia had seen everything, and been shocked by nothing—unimpressed, unexcited, unflinching, tired, permanent, and implacable.

"Not for long," Herman said.

"Thanks for putting me at ease," I said.

"Those kids have lost face," Herman said. "It's not about money any more."

"I'll be alert," I said. "You know anything about the woman?"

"Rikki? No. I hear she's a very snooty and spoiled broad, but it's just what I hear."

"Any reason you can think of why he wants me out of Port City?"

Herman shrugged. He smoked his cigarette without removing it from his mouth, so he had to squint a little to look through the smoke. As ash accumulated, he leaned over and tipped it off with his forefinger onto his empty plate.

"Nothing specific. It's not my turf. You'd have to figure there's something he don't want you to find out about."

"Know anything about the rackets in Port City?"

"Not really," Herman said. "Usual Chinatown stuff, I imagine. Extortion, gambling, heroin, prostitution, illegal immigrants."

"Chinese don't have a monopoly on most of that kind of thing," I said.

Herman smiled.

"They do in Chinatown," he said.

His cigarette was about to burn his lips. He spat it out and rummaged for another one.

"My mother used to call it the walking shadow."

"The tongs?" I said.

"The whole thing," Herman said. He lit another cigarette, put the Zippo away. "The whole thing. Wherever you went if you were Chinese, it followed you. Disappears when you shine a light on it. Move the light away, it's right there again, walking shadow."

He was looking past me out at the street, looking at the people moving past us, and they seemed to me for a minute as they must have seemed to Herman Leong all the time: insubstantial, and temporary wisps of momentary history that flickered past, while behind him was the

long, unchanging, overpowering weight of his race that
bore upon the illusory moment and overpowered it.

"You going back up there," Herman said.

"Yeah."

"Mistake."

I shrugged.

"I'm in the tough-guy business," I said. "I jump a case
because two teenagers tell me to fade, and what do I do
next for a living?"

Herman nodded.

"Guess you got to go back," he said.

"Yeah."

"Couple things," Herman said. "One, these kids are
absolute stone killers. Don't be thinking that they're
seventeen, or that they weigh about one hundred pounds.
Killing people is who they are. Makes them feel good."

I nodded.

"Same with anybody got nothing else," I said. "I'll
shoot one if I need to."

"You'll need to," Herman said. "And more than one."

"You said 'a couple of things.' What's the other?"

"Bring backup," Herman said. "I heard about you. And
I know about you even if I didn't. You're a cowboy."

I shrugged.

"You can't do this alone," Herman said.

I grinned.

"No man is an island," I said.

"Who said that, Hemingway?"

"John Donne, actually."

"Close enough," Herman said. *"Low faan* all look
alike, anyway."

chapter
18

I met Hawk in a parking lot behind the Port City Theater. It was drizzling, and the rain had made puddles on the uneven asphalt surface. Oil leaching into them made unpleasant-looking color spectrums on the surface of the dirty water. Hawk was wearing a black cowboy hat and a black leather trenchcoat, which he wore unbuttoned. He was leaning on his Jaguar, and beside him in a leather jacket and a tweed scally cap was Vinnie Morris.

"Vinnie," I said.

"Spenser."

"Assistance," Hawk said in his mock WASP accent, "in combating the yellow peril."

"You mention to Vinnie the fee?" I said.

"Told him he'd get what I'm getting."

"You back with Joe?" I said.

"No."

"Things are a little slow."

"Yeah. I got some dough put aside, but I'm sick of going over the dump every day, shooting rats."

"Good to keep your hand in," I said. "Hawk tell you the deal?"

"Un huh."

"Need to know anything else?"

"Who pays for my ammunition," Vinnie said.

"I do," I said. "It's a fringe benefit."

"Man, my career is taking off," Vinnie said.

The drizzle was becoming more insistent.

"We smart enough to get in out of the rain?" Hawk said.

"You bet," I said. "Want coffee?"

"Pick some place we don't like," Hawk said. "So it get shot up we won't feel bad."

"I got to meet Jocelyn Colby over here in something called the Puffin' Muffin."

"Fine."

Vinnie looked at Hawk.

"The Puffin' Muffin?" he said.

Hawk shrugged.

"Get used to it," he said.

The Puffin' Muffin, in the theater arcade, was one of the many shops in Port City designed for affluent Yankees, and located in places where affluent Yankees never went. When they did come, it was for an evening of theater at which time they were rarely hungry for muffins.

"Got a nice big picture window," Hawk said.

"Yeah."

"Let's not sit in it," Hawk said.

We took a seat against the rehabbed brick wall.

There was a counter across the back of the place and

a display case full of muffins. On the walls there were pictures of muffins; the pictures were interspersed with theater posters from the Port City Stage Company. The furniture was blond. Including the muscular waitress, with her long hair gathered in a geyser on top and tied with a pink ribbon. She poured us coffee from a thermos pot.

"Is it possible to get a muffin with my coffee?" I said.

She didn't smile. People never thought I was as funny as I did.

"Blueberry, bran, corn, banana, carrot, pineapple orange, cherry, raspberry, apple cinnamon, maple nut, lemon poppy seed, oat bran, cranberry, and chocolate chip," she said.

"Corn," I said.

"Toasted or plain?"

"Plain."

"Butter or margarine?"

"Neither."

"You want jelly with that?"

"No."

"Honey?"

"No."

She looked at the other two.

"Same," Hawk said.

Vinnie nodded.

The waitress went away.

"Any sign of anyone following Jocelyn?" I said.

Hawk grinned.

"Same guy following the Greek."

"You," I said.

"Un huh."

"Nobody else."

"Nobody," Hawk said.

The waitress came back with three corn muffins and put them down in front of us. She freshened our coffee.

"Can I get you anything else?" she said.

"No, thank you," I said.

She nodded and ripped a check from her pad and put it facedown on the table. Vinnie passed it to me.

"For crissake," I said, "ammunition and coffee?"

"I want the full ride," Vinnie said.

"It's working out good up here, isn't it," Hawk said.

"Yeah. If people weren't trying to shoot us, we'd have gotten nowhere."

I sampled my muffin.

"Long time no corn stalk," I said.

Across the room Jocelyn Colby came in wearing full foul-weather gear. She had on a long, yellow slicker, green rubber boots, and a green sou'wester with the brim turned up in front like a model in a cigarette ad. She saw me at the table and came straight over.

I introduced her to Vinnie. I could tell from her expression that she would have preferred to meet me alone. But she was a trouper.

"Have you caught him?" she said. She had big, violet eyes, with big lashes, and she knew it. She did a lot with them.

"We haven't seen him yet," I said.

The eyes widened.

"My God," she said. "He must have spotted you."

I nodded at Hawk.

"He didn't spot me," Hawk said.

Vinnie was looking for ways to improve his corn muffin. He broke off a piece and dunked it in his coffee, and ate it.

"Any improvement?" I said.

"Still tastes like a Frisbee," Vinnie said.

"Are you sure?" Jocelyn said to Hawk.

"Yes."

"Well, he's there. I've seen him."

"When did you see him last?" I said.

"Last night, after the play. He was there, in the shadows, at the corner of my street."

I looked at Hawk. He shook his head.

"You must have missed him," I said to Hawk.

"Sho 'nuff," Hawk said, his eyes full of amusement. Jocelyn wasn't looking at Hawk. She was giving me the all-out eye treatment.

"I'm frightened," she said to me.

"Of course you are, I don't blame you. He ever threaten you? Make any phone calls? Anything like that?"

"Yes. There've been . . . calls."

"What did he say?"

She shook her head.

"They were, ah, dirty. Vicious and dirty."

"Sexual threat?" I said.

"Yes. He said he was going to . . . do things to me."

I nodded. Hawk nodded. Vinnie was surveying the room. The waitress showed up and poured some coffee unasked into Jocelyn's cup.

"Want a muffin?" she said.

Jocelyn shook her head.

"We got bagels, you want some. Or we can make you some toast." Jocelyn shook her head.

"Frozen yogurt?"

Still studying the room, Vinnie said, "Beat it."

The waitress opened her mouth. Vinnie looked up at her. She closed her mouth and left. Jocelyn paid no attention. She was looking at me.

"How long have these threats been coming in?" I said.

"They just started. Just last night, after I went in the house, right after I saw him in the shadows."

"And could you describe him again?"

"Dark slouch hat, dark coat. He looks like the same one following Jimmy," she said. "I'm sure it's the same man. I'll bet it's someone jealous of Jimmy and me."

"You and Christopholous are an item?"

She looked down at the tabletop. She didn't say anything.

Hawk was looking at the door, his coat open, leaning back a little in his chair. Vinnie's jacket was unzipped. His eyes ranged the room. The only people besides us were two middle-aged women in sweat clothes sharing a dish of frozen strawberry yogurt. I waited. She was silent.

"You and Christopholous?" I said.

She shook her head.

"I didn't mean to say that."

I waited.

"I can't talk about it."

I waited some more. She raised her amazing eyes toward me and gave me the full charge.

"Please," she said. "I simply can't."

"Sure," I said.

Her eyes were very intense. "Imploring" was how she probably thought of it.

"You will protect me?" she said.

"Of course," I said. "We'll be there every minute."

"Could you, I mean no offense to anyone, but could you do it yourself."

"It would be my pleasure," I said. "We'll have to take turns, in fact. But it never hurts to demand the very best."

Hawk and Vinnie both glanced at me for a moment,

and then went back to looking around the room and watching the door.

"Are you on your way to the theater now?" I said.

"Yes."

"Then I'll start my shift now. I'll walk you there."

Hawk dropped a ten on top of the check.

"Big tip," Vinnie said.

"Reward for remembering all those muffins," Hawk said.

"They're coming too?" Jocelyn said.

"Just to watch," Hawk said. "Find out what makes him the very best."

"Won't do you any good," I said. "It's a white thing."

"Good," Vinnie said, and held the door open while Hawk went out and we followed him.

chapter
19

With Hawk and Vinnie behind us, Jocelyn and I strolled through the misting drizzle to the theater next door. She went in to rehearsal, and I went up to Christopholous' office on the second floor. Vinnie and Hawk lounged in the theater lobby, blending in to the theatrical scene like two coyotes at a poultry festival.

I sat in the chair across from Christopholous. The lights were on, making the day outside look even gloomier. The old brick office walls were bright with posters from previous Port City productions.

"Does Rikki Wu contribute a lot to the theater?" I said.

"A lot," Christopholous said. "And she holds an honored place on the board."

"A camel will pass through the eye of a needle more easily than a rich man will enter the kingdom of heaven," I said.

Christopholous grinned.

"That may be true of heaven," he said. "It is very much not true of a theatrical board of directors."

"The remark was sexist anyway," I said. "It should have been 'rich person.'"

"No doubt," Christopholous said. "Why do you ask?"

"Just to know," I said.

"But why do you want to know?"

"Because I don't. If I knew what was important to know, and what wasn't, I'd have this thing pretty much solved."

"Of course. Rikki's very generous. And very rich. Mr. Wu makes a great deal of money."

"Gee, the restaurant didn't look that busy," I said.

Christopholous shrugged.

"Perhaps he has other interests," he said.

"Like what?"

"Oh, God," Christopholous said. "I don't know. It was just an idle remark."

"Sure," I said. "How about Jocelyn Colby."

"Jocelyn?"

"Yeah. How do you and she get along."

"Jocelyn? Fine. She's a nice young woman. Limited in her acting skills, but ever compelling in the right role. Very attractive. Especially up close. The cheek bones. And those eyes. Film might actually be a better medium for her."

"You ever go out with her?" I said.

"Go out? You mean date?"

"Yeah."

"God, no," Christopholous said. "I could be her father."

"You've never had a, ah, relationship?"

"What the hell are you talking about. She's an actress

in a company I direct. She's a nice kid. She's around a lot. I like her. But, no, I've never even thought about having any kind of sexual relationship with her." Christopholous laughed. "You reach a certain age, and you discover that if you're going to talk with children, you'd rather they were your own."

"You have children?"

"Three," Christopholous said. "All of them older than Jocelyn."

"Wife?" I said.

"I divorced their mother, thank God, twenty years ago," Christopholous said. "What makes you ask about Jocelyn?"

"Same answer as above," I said. "Just accumulating data."

"But, I mean, are you asking everyone in the company if she went out with them? And why her in particular?"

I didn't want to tell him. I didn't know why, exactly. But one of Spenser's crime-stopper tips is: *You rarely get into trouble not saying stuff.* I shook my head vaguely.

"She have any romantic interest in anyone in the company?" I said.

"Jocelyn is, ah, affectionate. I don't follow the social interaction of my company too closely," Christopholous said. "But she did seem sort of interested in Lou."

"Montana? The Director?"

"Yes. I don't mean to suggest anything more than it was. She seemed for a while, when he first came aboard for *Handy Dandy,* to be especially interested in him. They'd have coffee together, and I know she called him a lot."

The day outside was cold enough to awaken the thermostat. I could hear the steam heat tingling in the pipes, still unwieldy from summer dormancy.

"What about him?" I said.

Christopholous smiled and shook his head.

"Ah, Lou," he said. "Life is imperfect. One must make do. Most of Lou's experience is in television."

"Ugh!" I said.

"Ugh, indeed," Christopholous said. "And worse, Lou is petty and pompous, and half as good as he thinks he is. But he can pull a play together. And at least while he is with us he appears to be committed to the company and to the rationale of the Theater Company. One cannot always hire the best Director. One must hire one who is willing to work for what one can pay."

"It is ever thus," I said, just to be saying something.

Christopholous shook his head.

"Not necessarily," he said. "In my experience, the actors are a bit different. Here we almost always get actors who care about the craft, about the art, if you will. It is in many ways a terrible profession. Sticking to it in the face of all the reasons to quit takes dedication and toughness. For most of them, the payoff is performing. The really good ones can always give a good performance despite the playwright or the Director, even in television or a dreadful movie."

"Olivier," I said.

"Yes, or Michael Caine."

"So, it's a kind of autonomy," I said.

"If they're good enough and tough enough," Christopholous said. "Interesting that you understand that so quickly; most people don't."

"I like autonomy," I said.

"I'm not surprised."

"Did Montana reciprocate any of Jocelyn's affection?"

"I'm not sure 'reciprocate' is the right word. He might have exploited it briefly."

"I've heard of that being done," I said.

"I wouldn't make too much of this," Christopholous said. "Jocelyn has her crushes, and they are as changeable as April weather."

"You know of any connection between her and the Wus?"

"The Wus? God, Spenser, you move too fast for me. Why would she have any connection with the Wus?"

"Why indeed," I said.

"Of course she knows Rikki. I want my company to shmooze the board members. It's part of the job."

"And one they savor," I said.

Christopholous shrugged.

"You have a goose laying a golden egg, you feed it," he said. "Rikki in particular enjoys being shmoozed."

"How about Mr. Wu?"

"He indulges her," Christopholous said. "That's really all I know about him. He comes very rarely to an event with her. When he does come he seems quite remote. But he seems willing to underwrite her without limit."

"He ever meet Jocelyn?"

"Oh, I wouldn't think so. Beyond a formal 'this-is-my-husband-Lonnie' kind of meeting. And if he had that, I'm sure he wouldn't register her. He never seems to be in the moment when he's here."

"I know the feeling," I said.

Through Christopholous' window I could see the rows of three-story clapboard houses, flat-roofed, mostly gray, mostly needing paint, with piazzas on the back. The piazzas were mostly devoid of furniture, except occasionally a dejected folding chair kept up the pretense. They seemed to be the place where people kept their trash. Clotheslines stretched across barren backyards at all three levels, but no clothes hung on them in the unyielding drizzle. The backyards grew a few weeds, unconnected and random in the mud.

"No further sign of your shadow?" I said.

"No, none. I guess you've scared him off."

"Something did," I said.

chapter
20

When I got to the lobby, Hawk was sitting on a bench against the wall, arms folded, feet thrust straight out, crossed at the ankles. The rain had made little impact on his polished cowboy boots. Vinnie was standing at the glass doors, looking out at the rain. He was a medium-sized guy with good muscle tone, and even features; and maybe the quickest hands I've ever seen. Hawk could catch flies with his hands. In fact, so could I. Vinnie could catch them between his thumb and forefinger. I sat beside Hawk. Vinnie kept staring out at the rain.

"Nobody following that broad," Hawk said.

"I know."

"We going to stay on her, anyway?"

"Yeah."

Hawk looked at me for a moment.

"Well, 'spite what everybody say, you not a moron."

"You're too kind," I said.

"I know. So I figure you going to follow her around for a while, see if she had any special reason for wanting you."

"And then I'll see what she does when I stop following her around," I said.

Hawk nodded.

"And then maybe we know something," he said.

"That'll be a nice change."

"Christopholous says he never had any kind of affair with her."

"She say he did."

"So we have a lie," I said.

"I'm betting it's the broad," Hawk said. "I think she wacko."

"She seems a better bet to be lying than Christopholous," I said. "But at least it's an allegation can be tracked. If they were romantically involved, somebody must have noticed."

"So you ask around."

"Yep. Christopholous says she was hot for the Director, Lou Montana."

"And me and Vinnie stay in the area, case the Chinks strike again."

"Asian Americans," I said.

"I forgot," Hawk said. "How much time you be spending in Cambridge?"

"Ever alert," I said, "for racial innuendo."

"Wasn't there a petition over there, keep the nigger kids out of that school on Brattle Street?"

"Of course," I said. "Everybody signed it, but no one ever called them niggers."

"Sensitive," Hawk said.

"Absolutely," I said. "Everybody knows words have the power to hurt."

"They do that."

Hawk grinned.

"But not like a kick in the balls," he said.

"No," I said. "Not like that."

We were quiet. Actors and stage technicians, dressed very informally, came and went through the lobby.

"So I'll follow Jocelyn a couple of days," I said. "Make her think I'm protecting her. And while she's rehearsing or whatever I'll ask around about her romantic interests, and you and Vinnie hang around in case the Chinks strike again."

"Good plan," Hawk said.

chapter
21

I stayed close to Jocelyn Colby for the rest of the week. Every morning when she came out of her apartment I was lurking somewhere out of sight: parked in my car up the street; strolling aimlessly by in the other direction; at a pay phone on the corner, talking animatedly to my answering machine. And all the time I did this, Hawk and Vinnie sat at a distance in Hawk's car and kept me in sight. I knew it was pointless. If there had been a shadow, Hawk would have spotted him. And the shadow would not have spotted Hawk. Hawk could track a salmon to its spawning bed without getting wet. But to make it work I had to pretend there was a shadow. So there I was in the rain, with the collar of my leather jacket turned up, and my hands in my pockets, and my black Chicago White Sox baseball cap pulled down over my forehead, staying alert for assassins, and pretending to shadow a shadow who didn't exist. My career did not seem to be taking off.

Friday, when Jocelyn came home from the theater, I didn't tail her. I walked with her. If Port City downtown was ever going to look good, which it wasn't, it was now. Mid-October, late afternoon when the light was nostalgic, and the endless drizzle made everything shiny. As we walked, Jocelyn put her hand lightly on my arm.

"How nice," she said. "I haven't been walked home in a long time."

"Hard to imagine," I said.

"Oh, it's brutal out there," she said. "Most men are such babies. The good-looking men you meet, the ones with manners and a little style, are gay. The straight ones are cheating on their wives. Or if they're single, they want to whine to you about their mother. Or their ex-wife."

"Where are all the good ones?" I said.

"God knows. Probably aren't any."

"I protest."

She laughed.

"I got a friend," she said, "insists that men are only good for moving pianos."

"They make good fathers, sometimes."

"And, the truth is," Jocelyn said, "I wouldn't mind if one galloped up and rescued me."

"From what?"

"From being a divorced woman without a guy," she said. "From being alone."

"Alone is not always such a bad thing," I said.

"You're not alone."

"No."

"You have Susan."

"Yes."

"So what the hell do you know," she said.

"I haven't always had Susan," I said.

"Yeah, well, I bet you didn't like that as much as you think you did."

"I prefer having her," I said.

We turned up Jocelyn's street. The cement sidewalk was buckled with frost heaves. The three-deckers crowded right up against the sidewalk, with no front yards. The blinds were drawn in their front windows. Their living rooms were a foot away from us as we walked along. She rummaged in her shoulder bag as we approached the house where she lived. It took her half a block of rummaging, but by the time we got to her door she had found her key.

"Thank you," she said. "You don't need to be here until ten tomorrow morning. I sleep late on Saturdays and Sundays."

"You don't need me here at all," I said. "There's no one following you."

She stopped with her key half into the lock. Her eyes were very wide.

"You have to come," she said.

"No," I said. "There's no one. If there were, Hawk or I would have caught him."

"He's not around because you are," she said. "If you leave, he'll be here."

"He didn't spot us," I said. "We're good at this."

"So what have you got going?" She sounded like an angry child. "You going away with Susan?"

"We're working on a house," I said.

"Fine. You're working on a house with *Susan.*" She made the name sound like it had many syllables. "And you don't give a goddamn what happens to me."

"You'll be swell," I said. "There's no one shadowing you."

"So." She stood with her hands on her hips now, the

key dangling untended in the lock. "You think I made it up."

"You tell me."

She was like a fourteen-year-old who'd been grounded. She talked with her teeth clenched.

"Prick master," she said.

"Wow," I said. "Prick master. I don't think anyone has ever called me that before."

"Well, you are a prick master," she said and turned the key in her door and wrenched it open and went in and slammed it shut.

Up the street Hawk pulled the Jaguar away from the curb and cruised up to the house and stopped. I got in the back. Vinnie was sitting up front beside Hawk with a shotgun between his knees. Hawk pulled the car away from the curb. The wipers moved at intervals back and forth across the windshield of the Jaguar. Hawk had the radio on softly playing.

"Still got that magic touch with the broads," Vinnie said to me. "Don't you."

"Just a spat," I said.

"She don't like it that you not coming tomorrow?" Hawk said.

"She called me a prick master," I said.

Vinnie half turned in the front seat and looked at me.

"Prick master?" he said. "I never heard that. Broad's pretty colorful."

At Hill Street, Hawk turned and headed up Cabot Hill. Vinnie was faced around front again and was looking out the car window at the near-empty street as we climbed away from the waterfront in the rain. He was chuckling to himself.

"Prick master," he said. "I like it."

chapter
22

Hawk waited until I went in the front door of my place on Marlboro Street before he pulled away. It was an old brownstone and brick townhouse, a block from the Public Garden, which had been turned into condominiums in the early eighties, when condos were high, and the living was easy. The lobby was done in beige marble. The oak stairway turned, in a series of angular landings, up around the open mesh elevator shaft.

Spry as ever, I skipped the elevator and took the stairs. I was wearing my New Balance running shoes with the aquamarine highlights and went up the stairs with very little noise, for a man carrying as much armament as I was. Since my visit from Lonnie and the Dreamers I felt I needed more fire power. I was wearing the Browning .9 mm on my hip with a round in the chamber and 13 in the clip. I also had the .357 butt forward on the left side of my belt with six rounds in the cylinder. I had decided against a blunderbuss.

My place was on the second floor, and as I turned toward my door down the hall past the elevator shaft, I smelled cigarette smoke. I stopped. I sniffed. I checked the elevator shaft. The car was at the top, resting quietly on the sixth floor. My place occupied the whole second floor. The smell of cigarette smoke was from my place. It was a fresh smell, not the stale remnant of a cigarette long since smoked, but the fresh smell of one just lit, drawn in deeply and exhaled. I looked at my door. There was no change in the way light shone through the peep hole. I took the Browning off my hip, and cocked it and walked quietly back down the short hall to the stairwell behind the elevator shaft.

Susan was the only one with a key and she didn't smoke. If someone had Murphied the lock they were good at it, because there was no sign of it on the door jamb. There was a fire escape near my kitchen window, which could have been used for access. The way they got in was less significant for the moment than the fact that they were in there.

It could, of course, be the tooth fairy copping a quick lungful before slipping a quarter under my pillow, but it was more likely to be a couple of gunnies sent by Lonnie Wu, and if it was, in addition to myself, I wanted one alive.

The stairwell was silent. The elevator remained motionless on the top floor. I was the only one, normally, who used the stairs. People on the first floor obviously had no need, people from the third floor up always took the elevator. However they had gotten in, there were two ways out. There was the fire escape, which came down into the public alley between Marlboro and Beacon

Street. And there was the front door. I could cover the alley from Arlington Street. I could cover the front door from the stairwell. Backup would have helped.

The sounds of a silent building are always surprising when you are standing quiet and listening hard. There is the tiny creak of the building's constant struggle with gravity and stress, the cycling of heat and ventilation, the faint hint of refrigerators or personal computers, a murmur, almost imaginary, of television sound, and compact discs. From outside come sounds of traffic, and wind, and the audible, celestial hush of the world moving through space.

I knew I could outwait them. I could outwait Enoch Arden if I had to. But it would be nice if, when they finally got sick of waiting, I knew which way they'd exit. I didn't know how long they'd been there. If they were the two kids I'd seen with Lonnie Wu, they wouldn't have much patience. Kids never do, and Lonnie's two jitterbugs probably had a lot less than most. They might be ready to leave now. If I went for backup, I might lose them. And I didn't want to.

There was a skylight at the top of the stairwell, but the late October afternoon had blended with the late October evening and the stairwell was lit only by the dim bulbs near the elevator door on each floor. No light showed through the peep hole in my door. *The evening stretches out against the sky,* I thought. *Like a patient etherized upon a table.* I grinned to myself. *Live fast, die young, and have a literate corpse.*

On the sixth floor I heard the elevator door slide open slowly. There was a moment when nothing happened, and then the elevator jerked into life and came slowly down past me. On the first floor the doors slid open.

There were footsteps. The front door opened. And closed.

I kept my eyes on the door to my apartment. After fifteen or twenty minutes it becomes harder than you'd think it would be. But I had spent half my life looking at things for too long a time, and had learned how. The door didn't open. I continued to look at it. I no longer smelled the cigarette smoke. My nose had gotten used to it. If I hadn't quit smoking twenty-five years ago, I'd probably have opened my front door without noticing anything and walked right into a bullet with others following hard upon. Further argument to confound the Tobacco Institute.

I hadn't figured out how to get them out of there, and I hadn't figured out what to do if they went out the fire escape. So I stayed with Spenser's crime-stopper tip number 7. When uncertain of what to do, hang around. I leaned on the corner of the elevator shaft and looked at my door. Nothing happened.

I speculated on the sexual potential of an anchorwoman I liked on local television. I decided that it was considerable. As was my own. I considered whether sexual speculation about a prominent female newsperson was sexist and concluded that it was. I wondered if she looked good with her clothes off. I reminded myself that anyone who looked good with clothes on would, of course, look even better with clothes off.

I shrugged my shoulders and bent my neck in an effort to loosen my traps. I did some calf raises. I opened and closed my left hand twenty times and then shifted the Browning into it and opened and closed my right hand twenty times. Then I shifted the Browning back.

Somebody in the building was cooking onions. I was hungry. I had expected to come home, have a drink, and

cook myself supper. I had not expected to find one or
more nicotine slaves in my way. I was going to make
myself some shredded pork barbecue out of a pork
tenderloin I had in the refrigerator. I was going to serve
it with red beans and rice, coleslaw on the side, and some
corn bread, which I was going to make from Crutchfield
self-rising white corn meal. Instead I was standing out
here in the dark trying to keep my extremities from going
to sleep and listening to my stomach growl.

Being a hero was not an unencumbered pleasure.

I tried compiling a list of things I liked best—dogs, jazz,
beer, women, working out, ball games, books, Chinese
food, paintings, carpentry. I would have included sex, but
everyone included sex, and I didn't want to be common. I
thought about my comics hall of fame. Alley Oop, Li'l
Abner, Doonesbury, Calvin and Hobbes, Tank McNamara,
of course. . . . I was sick of waiting. . . . I shifted the
Browning to my left hand and took the .357 from my belt
with my right. I cocked it, and stepped out from behind
the elevator shaft, and fired one round from the revolver
through my front door. Then I fired three rounds from the
Browning and another round from the .357. Then I
hotfooted it down the front stairs and out the front door.
I went down Marlboro Street on the dead run with a gun
in each hand, turned the corner on Arlington Street, past
one building and into the alley that ran behind my
building.

It was dark. I flattened against the wall behind a
bulkhead that sheltered some trash barrels. I could hear
my heart pumping hard, trying to catch up with my
sudden sprint. In the cool October night I could feel the
sweat drying on my face. The side of my building caught
some moon glow. If it had worked, they should be on the
fire escape. I forced myself to look wide-eyed and

unfocused at the whole side of my building, rather than trying to concentrate. In the dark you saw better if you did it that way. Especially movement. Like the movement on the fire escape below my window. Two figures coming down. *Ah, Spenser,* I thought, *you tricky devil, you've done it again!* I would have been even more impressed with myself if it hadn't taken me an hour to think of this ploy.

The two figures dropped to the ground and started down the alley toward Arlington Street. One of them was putting his gun away inside his coat. They came quietly down the alley, not running, but moving quickly and staying in the shadows. They passed from the pale moon light into the shadows, and their eyes took a moment to adjust. They passed me in the shadows without any notice. They looked like the two kids who'd come with Lonnie Wu and scared me to death. I stepped out behind them, grabbed one of them by the hair, and jammed the Browning into his ear. I didn't say anything. They probably didn't speak English. And I didn't know how to say "Stick 'em up" in Chinese. The kid grunted and his buddy turned with his gun out. I kept myself behind my teeny bopper, so his pal couldn't get a shot at me. The pal began to back down the alley toward Arlington Street, in a crouch, gun forward, held in both hands, looking for a shot at me and not able to get one. I was afraid he'd shoot at me anyway and kill his buddy. These were not stable young men. I took my gun out of the kid's ear and waved it at the other one, making a "beat it" gesture. For a moment, we faced off that way. The kid I had hold of tried to twist out of the way, but I was much too big and strong for him, and I kept him jammed against me, his head yanked back against my chest. In the distance was the sound of a siren. Somebody in my building had probably objected to gunshots in the stairwell, and called the cops. My neighbors were so traditional. The kid heard the siren, and for another moment held his crouch despite it. Then he broke, and turned, and ran. At the corner of Arlington Street, he turned toward Boylston Street, and disappeared. I didn't care about him. I had one, which was all I needed.

chapter
23

I sat in an interrogation room at Police Headquarters with
Herman Leong and the Vietnamese shooter.

"Name's Yan," Herman said.

"He speak any English?" I said.

The room was cinder block painted industrial beige.
The floor was brown tile and the suspended ceiling was
cellotex tile that had started out white. The door was oak
with yellow shellac finish. There were no windows.
Light came from a fluorescent fixture that hung from
short lengths of chain in the center of the room.

"Probably," Herman said. "But he won't let on."

Herman sat beside me on one side of an oak table
shellacked the same yellow as the door. A lot of
cigarettes had left their dark impressions on its edges.
The kid sat across the table on a straight chair. He wore
a white shirt buttoned to the neck, and dark, baggy

trousers. His black hair was long, and it hung over his forehead and down to the corners of his eyes. He said something to Herman. Herman shook his head.

"Wants a cigarette," Herman said.

"Tell him he'll get one just before the blindfold."

Herman nodded and didn't say anything. The kid stared at me. His eyes were black and empty.

"How old is he?" I said.

Herman spoke to him. Yan answered. His voice was uninflected. His face blank. He looked bored.

"Says he thinks he's seventeen. He doesn't know for sure."

I nodded.

"Why do you ask?" Herman said.

"Just wondered," I said.

"He's old enough to kill you," Herman said. "You let him."

"I won't let him," I said. "What was he doing in my apartment?"

I waited for the translation.

"Says he wasn't in your apartment."

"We'll be able to make him there," I said. "There'll be prints."

Herman translated. Yan shrugged.

"What was he doing on the fire escape?" I said to Herman. Herman spoke to Yan. Yan answered.

"Says he was just climbing it for the hell of it, was coming down when you jumped him in the alley for no reason."

"How come he was carrying a .45-caliber automatic pistol?"

"Says he found it and was going to take it to the police."

I looked at Yan, and smiled. He stared back at me blankly.

"Tell him," I said, "that we've got him for carrying a handgun without a license. We've got him for breaking and entering."

Yan said something to Herman.

"Yan says you can't prove he was breaking in anyplace."

"He's on the fire escape outside my open window," I said. "We'll lift some prints that will place him in my apartment. He's looking at a couple of felonies."

Yan smiled faintly and looked at Herman while Herman translated. His smile widened a little as he listened. Then he spoke very fast to Herman.

"Says you must be on something. Says his lawyer's going to show up inside of an hour and he's going to walk. Says the streets are crowded with people got busted on worse than what you got. Says you're an asshole."

"What's the Chinese word for asshole?" I said.

Herman smiled.

"Loose translation," he said.

"He from Port City?"

"Says he's not from anywhere. Just drifting."

"He a Death Dragon?" I said.

"Says no."

"Who sent him to kill me?" I said.

Herman spoke for a while. The kid said a word. Herman spoke again. The kid shrugged.

"Nobody," Herman said.

"He have an ID on him?"

"No."

"How long has he been here?"

"He's not sure. He came when he was small."

"And he still doesn't speak English?"

Herman spoke. Yan spoke. Herman spoke. Yan almost smiled. He looked at me and said something.

"Says nobody he knows speaks English. Says you're the first white person he ever talked to."

"Who better?" I said.

Herman looked straight at Yan as he spoke to me.

"He may know a few English words. He may know enough to follow our conversation. But it's no advantage to him to let you know. He's got no family, or if he does it works all the time, and has no control over him. He may be lying about his age. He may be fourteen for all we know. He's alone in a foreign land where no one understands his language. What he's got is the gang. If he's who we think he is, it's probably the Death Dragons in Port City. The gang is who and what he is. He finks to you and he hasn't even got that any more."

I nodded.

"Plus they'll kill him," I said.

Yan looked at me silently. It wasn't a pose. He was like a feral child. His silence was visceral. Nearly inert, he was beyond threatening, or bribing, or scaring.

"Un huh," Herman said.

"What kind of life is that?" I said.

"It's the life he's got, Spenser. Don't get all gooey about it. You'd walked into your place he'd have put half a dozen .45-caliber slugs in your face. And liked it."

I nodded again.

"Any feeling is better than no feeling," I said.

Yan and I looked at each other. Between us was an immeasurable ocean of silence.

"Yan," I said, slowly, as if he could understand me, "I know, and you know, and you know I know that Lonnie Wu sent you and the other kid to clip me. I resent it. I am going to find out why Lonnie sent you, and I'm going to take him down for it, and you are probably going to go too."

Yan had no reaction. I nodded at Herman. Herman translated. Yan had no reaction. The door to the interrogation room opened and a uniformed cop stuck his head in.

"Lawyer's here to get him," the cop said.

Herman looked at me.

"Want me to leave you two alone for a few minutes?" Herman said. "While I stall the lawyer?"

I studied the kid in front of me for a moment. His wrists were slimmer than Susan's. He couldn't have weighed more than 130.

"No."

Herman shrugged. He pointed a finger at Yan, then at the cop. He said something in Chinese. The boy stood and walked to the door. He stopped for a moment and stared back at me without expression. I aimed a forefinger at him, cocked my thumb, and dropped it like the hammer on a pistol. Yan turned and left with the cop. I looked at Herman.

"Lucky I was able to grab him," I said.

"Yeah," Herman said. "Otherwise you'd never have been able to question him."

"And I wouldn't have known his name was Yan."

"I forgot that," Herman said. "You did learn something."

"Unless he was lying," I said.

"You going to be fucking around with the Kwan Chang tong," Herman said. "You are doing some industrial-strength fucking around, you know? They got a hundred kids like Yan, be happy to kill you, and don't care if you kill them too. You got any backup?"

"I got some."

"Anybody I know?"

"Hawk's with me," I said.

Herman nodded.

"Figures," he said.

"And Vinnie Morris."

"Vinnie? I thought he was with Joe Broz."

"They split, couple years ago."

"Well, he's good. Who else you got?"

"That's it."

"You, Hawk, and Vinnie Morris?"

"All three," I said. "Doesn't seem fair to the tong, does it?"

chapter
24

We were on lunch break in Concord. Pearl had located a crow at the very top of a large white pine, and was pointing it with quivering immobility. Paw up, nose extended, tail straight out, every part of her shouting soundlessly, "There's a bird."

"Want me to shoot it for her?" Vinnie said. A .12-gauge pump gun was leaning on the picnic table.

"No," Susan said. "She's gun-shy."

"What you got for load in there?" Hawk said.

"Fours."

"Won't leave much bird," Hawk said.

"I didn't load it for birds," Vinnie said.

Hawk grinned and pointed at him.

"Please don't misunderstand," Susan said. "I think you're lovely company. But why are you here? With shotguns?"

Hawk and Vinnie looked at me.

"That's a rifle," Hawk said, nodding at the Marlin .30/30 leaning on the table. "Need some range out here in the damn forest."

"Some Chinese people in Port City are mad at me," I said.

"Chinese people?"

"Specifically Rikki Wu's husband," I said.

"Lonnie?"

"Un huh."

"And you need Hawk and Vinnie for protection from Lonnie Wu?"

"Lonnie Wu is a mobster," I said. "He's connected to the Kwan Chang tong, which runs all things Chinese north of New Haven."

Susan stared at me.

"Rikki's husband?"

"Un huh."

"You never ask for help."

"Hardly ever," I said.

"This is bad," she said.

"Yeah."

"Have there been any, ah, incidents?"

"Two," I said. I told her about them.

Susan was quiet, listening, and when I got through, she remained quiet. Beyond the yard trees, and the meadow, down the slope, beyond the stream, the hardwoods had shed all of their leaves, as if simultaneously. Past them, in the distance, other trees had not yet begun unleaving, and they remained bright and various behind the bare, gray spires, punctuated by the thick evergreens. The crow flew away, and Pearl, after a brief dash in the direction of its flight, turned her attention back to our lunch.

"It's what you do," Susan said. "I've always known it. And I've come to terms with it."

Pearl put her head on Vinnie's lap, her eyes rolled up looking at the smoked turkey sandwich that Vinnie was eating.

"But it scares me."

"Sure," I said.

"And I want you to be as careful as you can be . . . and not let them kill you."

"None of us want that to happen," I said.

Hawk seemed not to be listening—which was an illusion. Hawk always knew everything that was going on around him. He was looking at the road, and then at the meadow, and down toward the woods, and back at the road.

Vinnie was staring down at Pearl as he chewed his sandwich. She stared back up at him. He scowled at her. She continued to stare at his sandwich. Finally he pulled off a corner of the sandwich and gave it to her. She raised her head, swallowed it, put her head back in his lap and continued to gaze at the sandwich.

"Swell," Vinnie said.

"Do you think that Lonnie is connected to Craig Sampson's murder?" Susan said.

"He could be connected," I said. "Or it could be something else."

"Like?"

"Like he's running some rackets in town and he doesn't want an outsider coming in, stumbling across them, and causing trouble."

"But isn't trying to kill you the wrong way to do that?" Susan said. "If he's covering up something, wouldn't that just cause more attention to be brought?"

"I've thought about that," I said. "And I've got a couple of conclusions."

Vinnie got careless with his sandwich, and Pearl snapped the rest of it out of his hand and sped away to finish it off. I pushed another sandwich toward Vinnie.

"Ever occur to you maybe I don't like dogs?" Vinnie said.

"It has," I said.

"Isn't she quick?" Susan said.

"Quick," Vinnie said, and unwrapped his new sandwich. Pearl came back to the table and looked at Susan and wagged her tail. Susan bent over and gave her a kiss on the muzzle.

"Good for you," she said to Pearl. Then she looked at me and said, "Conclusions?"

"The first time they made a run at me was in Port City, in a public place, middle of the day," I said.

"Like maybe they weren't sweating the Port City Police Department," Hawk said, his gaze moving comfortably over the landscape.

"And the second time," I said, "they were in Boston, and if they'd have succeeded, who would tie it to Port City?"

"And even if somebody did," Hawk said, "maybe they still not sweating Port City Police."

"Hawk has reached the same conclusions," I said to Susan.

"I still say if it were me, I'd just lie low and await developments."

"Sure," I said. "But a guy like Lonnie, he's used to doing what he wants to. He's an activist. And, he may have people to answer to. Maybe he gets a call from the head guy at Kwan Chang—'get the white guy out of our town.' Say Hawk's right and he's wired with the cops.

There's not a lot of risk. And he doesn't know I'm stubborn. So he warns me, and it doesn't work. How's he look now? He can't run Port City the way they want it, then the tong will replace him. And he's going to run the Death Dragons, he can't lose face by letting me ignore him."

Susan nodded.

"So it makes sense from Lonnie's point of view," she said. "But we still don't know whether he's involved in Craig's death."

"No, we don't."

"And we have no idea who was shadowing Jimmy?"

"No, we don't."

"And Jocelyn."

"About her I've got an idea."

Susan smiled at me.

"Oh, good," she said.

"Yes," I said. "It's a start."

Pearl scrambled up on the benchseat between me and Susan and sat at table hopefully. Susan put her arm around her.

"You went to Harvard," I said. "If I needed a translator, you think you could find one?"

"I imagine so," Susan said.

"I don't want a specialist in ritual folk poetry of the Tang Dynasty," I said. "I need someone who can talk to street types."

"I sort of guessed that," Susan said.

"Wow," I said. "You did go to Harvard."

Hawk speared two bread and butter pickles from the open jar, gave one to Pearl, and ate the other one. Pearl swallowed hers and waited. Nothing happened so she bounced up onto the table and put her nose in the jar. The mouth of the jar was too small and she couldn't get it all the way in, but she was able to put her tongue in and lap a little pickle juice. Vinnie watched in silence.

"Fucking dog's up on the fucking table eating the pickles," he said.

Susan smiled at him patiently.

"She likes pickles," Susan explained.

chapter
25

Hawk and Vinnie were sitting with me in my office with the door locked to keep the Death Dragons at bay. We were drinking some coffee and eating some donuts. Hawk was reading a book by Cornel West, and Vinnie was sitting with his feet up on the corner of my desk and his eyes half closed, listening to his Walkman through the earphones. I had some mail to go through, and then I had to think about Port City. Most of the mail was junk. And so was most of what I knew about Port City. Vinnie was humming softly to himself. Hawk looked up from his book.

"What you listening to?" he said.

"Lennie Welch," Vinnie said.

Hawk looked blank.

Vinnie gave him a sample. "'You-oo-oo-oo made me leave my happy home . . .'"

"Lucky you can shoot," Hawk said and went back to his book.

Someone turned the knob on my office door. Hawk rolled left out of his chair, Vinnie went right. They came to their feet on either side of the door, guns out, hammers back. Vinnie was still wearing the Walkman. I was crouching behind the desk, with the Browning aimed at the door.

"Yeah?" I said.

"Spenser? Lee Farrell, is this a bad time?"

I put the gun away and nodded at Hawk to open the door. He did, and Lee walked in. He looked at Hawk and Vinnie still on either side of the door.

"Hawk," he said.

"Lee."

"Vinnie Morris," I said. "Lee Farrell."

Lee nodded at him.

Vinnie said, "I know he ain't a Chink, but he's wearing a gun."

"He's a cop," I said.

Vinnie shrugged, and went back and sat down. Hawk locked the door again and leaned on the wall. Lee looked around.

"You expecting trouble?"

"Just because the door's locked and I've got a couple guys with me."

"Guys? I know Hawk, and I've heard of Vinnie Morris."

I grinned.

"When you care enough to get the very best," I said.

"Yeah," Lee said.

He took a donut out of the box on my desk and ate some.

"I'm on my way to work," he said. "I ran Craig

Sampson's name through Triple I, and he's not there. So I queried the FBI and they have him."

"Why wasn't it in the Triple I index?"

"Nobody's perfect," Lee said.

"Is it his prints from the army? Or something else?"

"I don't know. I requested his file."

"And?"

"Their computer's backed up, they'll get to it."

"How soon?"

"FBI is a federal agency," Farrell said. "How soon would you figure?"

"Not soon," I said.

"That's about when I figure. You got a fax?"

"Of course not," I said. "I just got an answering machine."

"Yeah, silly question. I'll drop it off when it gets here. You taken up firearms yet, or do you still carry a pike?"

"I like a pike," I said. "But it screws the line of my sport coat."

Lee stood. He looked at Hawk and at Vinnie.

"You seem in pretty good shape," he said. "But, you need some extra backup, give me a shout."

"Thanks," I said.

chapter
26

I'd caught a large corporation in a big insurance scam last year and been awarded ten percent by the insurance company. I'd put most of it into the house in Concord, and the rest of it into a Mustang convertible, because I thought it would be dandy to solve crimes with the wind blowing through my hair. It was red and had a white roof, and when Susan was with me, I had to keep the top up because it messed her hair. And when Pearl was with me I had to keep the top up because she was inclined to jump out every time she saw a cat. And when I took it to Port City I had to keep the top up because it was always raining. The wipers worked good though, and I didn't seem to be solving crimes, anyway.

I went off the highway at Hill Street and wound down toward the waterfront, descending as I went lower into the Port City social strata. Hawk sat in the front seat beside me and Vinnie Morris was in back.

"Got a plan for today, Cap'n?" Hawk said.

"When all else fails," I said, "investigate."

"You mean clues and shit?" Vinnie said.

"Yeah. I need to look at Sampson's apartment, and show his picture to people, and go to bars, and stores, and movie theaters, and restaurants and ask people if they ever saw him, and if they did, who was he with."

"How come you didn't do that right off?" Vinnie said.

"Hawk?" I said.

"'Cause the police do police work better than he do," Hawk said. "'Cause they got a lot of bodies available to do it. And he only got him."

"That would be a problem," Vinnie said. "So why do it now? Because that Boston cop told you about the FBI prints?"

"Yeah," I said. "DeSpain told me that they had no history on him. Said there was no record of Sampson's prints."

"DeSpain?" Vinnie said. "Used to be a state cop named DeSpain."

"Same guy," I said.

"DeSpain was good," Vinnie said. "Tough bastard, but good."

"So either he's not good any more or he was lying to me," I said.

"So you gotta go over all the ground you thought he'd cover."

"Un huh."

"This is likely to annoy Lonnie Wu," Hawk said.

"Maybe," I said.

"And maybe DeSpain."

"Maybe."

"And maybe somebody do something we can catch them at," Hawk said.

"That would be nice."

"'Less they shoot your ass," Hawk said.

"You and Vinnie are supposed to prevent that," I said.

"And if we don't?" Vinnie said.

"You don't like the plan," I said. "I'm open to suggestions."

"Hey," Vinnie said. "I don't fucking think. I just shoot people."

"Sooner or later," Hawk said.

We reached the street where Sampson's apartment was, and turned into it and parked on a hydrant in front of his building.

"It'll probably take me a while," I said.

"Probably will," Hawk said.

I put a small flashlight in my pocket, and one of those multi-combination survival tools, and got out of the car into the pleasant steady rain. Hawk got behind the wheel and Vinnie came up in the front seat. Hawk shut off the lights and the wipers and turned off the motor. The rain immediately collected on the windows, and I couldn't see them any more.

I turned and walked toward the house where Craig Sampson had lived. It was three stories, gray, black shutters, white trim. There was a front porch four steps up, and a front door painted black. Narrow, full-length windows framed the front door. The windows were dirty. There were shabby lace curtains in them. The housepaint had blistered away leaving long, bare patches, but the wood beneath was gray with age and soil so that it nearly matched.

There were three door bells. The first two had names in the little brass frames beneath. The top frame was empty. I peered in through the murky glass past the ratty curtains. There was a narrow hallway, an interior door on the right, and a staircase rising along the right wall beyond it. I tried the front door. It was locked. I looked at the doorbells. There was no intercom associated with them. I rang all the doorbells and waited. Inside the house the first floor door opened, and a thin, angry-looking woman opened the front door. I checked the name on the first floor bell.

"Hello," I said. "Ms. Rebello?"

"What's your story," she said. She was nearly as tall as I was, and high-shouldered, and narrow. Her hair was about the color of the house and tightly permed. She was wearing a flowered dress and sneakers. The little toe of her right sneaker had been cut out, presumably to relieve pressure on a bunion.

"You the landlady?" I said.

She nodded. I took out my wallet and opened it and flashed my gun permit at her. It had my picture on it, and looked official. She squinted at it.

"Police," I said. "I need to take another look at Craig Sampson's apartment."

I closed my wallet and stowed it. I knew she had no idea what she had just looked at.

"Well, I wish you'd be a little neater this time," she said. "I'm going to have to rent that place."

"Lady, my heart bleeds," I said. "All I got to think about is how somebody shot your tenant full of holes."

I figured nice didn't work with her.

"Yeah, well, you already looked once," she said. "And I got no rent coming in from the place."

I nodded and jerked my thumb up the stairs.

"Just unlock the deceased's door," I said.

Still muttering, she turned and walked up the stairs ahead of me, limping on her bunion.

"I got a mortgage to pay . . . I don't get income out of this place, I still got to pay the mortgage . . . Bank don't care who got killed, or who didn't. I don't pay the mortgage, I'm out in the street . . . You people just take your own sweet damn time about it. . . . What am I supposed to do with his stuff, anyway?"

At the third floor there was a tiny landing, lit by a 60-watt bulb in a copper-tone sconce. She took some keys from the pocket of her house coat and fumbled at the lock.

"Don't even have my glasses," she said. "Can't see a damn thing without them."

She finally found the keyhole and opened the door and stepped aside.

"Close the door when you leave," she said. "Downstairs too. They'll lock behind you."

"Sure," I said and stepped past her into the apartment and closed the door. I listened for a moment and heard her limp back down the stairs. Then I turned my attention to the apartment.

chapter
27

There was a bathroom directly opposite the front door, a two-stride hallway to the right that led into a bed-sitting room with a huge black-and-white theater poster filling the far wall, and some gray light coming in wearily from the single dormer window. The poster was of Brando in *A Streetcar Named Desire*. The bed was one of those oak platform deals with storage drawers underneath. There was a green Naugahyde arm chair, and a gray metal desk and chair. At the foot of the bed was a gray metal foot locker. The walls were white, but an old white and one that hadn't been washed very often.

I could hear the rain on the roof. I looked out of the one window for a moment and watched the rain fall gently past me and down three stories and onto the roof of my convertible. The rain had hurried the fall of leaves along the street. They plastered the roadway with limp,

green-tinged yellow spatters, and collected in the storm
culverts and backed up the water. A gray and white
municipal bus moved past, sending spray up from the
puddles onto the sidewalk. I turned back to the room.
Everything was neat. Ms. Rebello had probably stepped
in after the cops had tossed it. Funny they should have
left it messy. Usually they don't.

I started at the bathroom and went through the room
slowly. Even in a bath-and-bed apartment there are lots
of places to look when you don't know what you're
looking for. I looked under the rug and in the toilet tank.
I felt inside the water spout in the tub. I used the plier
part of my combination tool to take off the shower head.
I pulled the stopper from the drain and shined my
flashlight in. I shook out the towels, and felt carefully
over the shower curtain. I checked the tiles in the shower
to make sure there wasn't a loose one with something
hidden behind it. I did the same with the baseboard, and
the ceiling molding. I removed the nut from the tap in the
sink drain and found a wet soap-and-hair ball. I didn't
know what I was looking for, but I knew that wasn't it.
I shined my light into the sink drain. I emptied the
wastebasket and put the stuff back in. I smelled the
shaving lotion and looked at the bottle against the light.
I tasted the baby powder and then emptied the container
into the toilet. There was nothing in there but talc. I
flushed the toilet and threw the container in the wastebasket. I held the shampoo bottle up to the light. I
examined the toothpaste tube, and the deodorant stick
and the shaving cream can. All of them were what they
appeared to be. I took the toilet paper off the roll and
looked at it carefully from each end. There was nothing
rolled into it. I shined my light between each vane on the
radiator. I checked the medicine cabinet. When I was

satisfied that there was nothing that would do me any good in the bathroom, I moved to the big room. And in about ten minutes I found it.

Taped to the bottom of one of the storage drawers in the platform bed was a white envelope and in the envelope were eight Polaroid pictures, seven of a woman with no clothes on, one, taken in a mirror, of a man and woman with no clothes on. The man was Craig Sampson. The woman was holding a towel in front of her face.

I took the pictures over to the desk and sat down and spread them out on the desk and turned on the gooseneck lamp that sat on the back corner of the desk. I studied them in an entirely professional way. She was lying on, or standing beside, a bed in what was probably a hotel room. She was either stark naked (five pictures, including the one with Sampson) or wearing the kind of garter belt and stockings get-up that has so successfully weathered the test of time in *Playboy* (three pictures). I was comforted by the garter belt poses. I'd begun to think only Hef and I still cared for that sort of thing.

The room was very still while I looked at the pictures. There was the white sound of the rain on the roof, the occasional settling creak of an old house responding to the steady weight of gravity, and an occasional sound of steam heat knocking tentatively in the pipes.

The woman looked as if she exercised often. Her body was firm, and her stomach was flat. With the towel always concealing her features, there was nothing to tell me who she was. Well, not quite nothing. Though it was hard to be sure in a Polaroid, she appeared to have no body hair. Theoretically this oddity would be an excellent identity clue. But it was of limited practical value.

The pictures didn't have to mean much. Lots of people liked to take nude pictures of themselves and their partners. Some of them even concealed their face. Still it told me that Sampson had a relationship which he concealed. No one knew of it. Everyone said he had no girlfriends. And the fact that this girlfriend concealed her identity was at least mildly interesting. What was more interesting was that the cops had missed it. It wasn't that hard to find, and any cop would know to look under a drawer when searching a place. These cops had searched it so thoroughly that they'd made a mess, and they hadn't found these pictures?

It gave one pause. But here was not the place for pausing. I put the pictures back in the envelope and put the envelope in my inside jacket pocket, and went through the rest of the room. I unmade the bed and remade it. I felt under every drawer, behind the poster, all the usual moves, and didn't find anything else that mattered. I put everything back carefully. I was neat and polite and generally swell, for a gumshoe. But it is also easier to search a place if you don't make a mess. You're not pawing through the jumble you just created.

I left Sampson's room, pulled the door shut and heard it latch behind me. Then I went down the two dark flights of narrow stairs and knocked on Ms. Rebello's door. She must have been making late breakfast or early lunch. I could smell bacon cooking in there. I did not think it cooked for me.

The door opened on the safety chain.

"Yuh?"

"I wish to take action on this," I said. "Just how messy were the police who searched that room earlier?"

"Messy," she said. "A couple goddamn pigs, excuse my French."

"Emptied out drawers, that sort of thing?"

"Clothes all over the floor. Papers, bedclothes. Pigs."

"Well, they're going to regret it," I said.

"That all?" she said. "Can I pack the place up and rent it?"

"Absolutely," I said. "And please accept my apologies for the mess and the delay as well."

"Yeah," she said, "sure," and closed the door.

I smiled to myself in the ugly little hall. *Got to take fun where you find it.* I went out the front door and pulled it carefully shut behind me and heard the latch click. I glanced up and down the street. There was no one in sight. In front of the house my car started with a small puff of smoke from the exhaust and the window washers began to move. I turned the collar up on my leather jacket, and went down the four front steps into the rain, and across the sidewalk and into my car.

"Any luck?" Hawk said.

"I don't know," I said.

I took out the nude pictures and passed them around.

"The guy Sampson?" Vinnie said.

"Yeah."

"Know the woman?"

"No."

"She's got no pussy," Vinnie said.

"Observant," I said.

"And eloquent," Hawk said.

Neither Vinnie nor Hawk had anything meaningful to contribute to the absent body hair question. There was a lively discussion of nude women we had known. The consensus was that, while body hair varied considerably, none of us had ever known anyone with none. Vinnie handed me back the pictures, and I put them back in my pocket.

"Better count them," Hawk said, and put the car in drive and eased away from the curb.

chapter
28

Ocean Street in Port City starts at the foot of Hill Street and runs parallel to the harbor for maybe a mile and a half, before it curves around an inlet and turns into Seaside Drive. One on each side of the street, Hawk and I started at the south end, near the theater, and began to ask people if they knew Craig Sampson. We each had a publicity still from the theater to show. We kept an eye on each other as we worked, and Vinnie dawdled along behind us in the car with a shotgun leaning against the front passenger seat.

The Port City Tap was my fifth stop. On a wet afternoon it was a haven of good cheer. Three guys were sitting at the bar not talking to each other, and a woman wearing a black cowboy hat, with a big feather, was in a booth by herself with a stack of quarters in front of her on the table next to something that looked like a strawberry soda, but probably wasn't. The jukebox was playing some kind of country western music that sounded to me like a chicken being strangled, though Susan would probably have liked it. A television set above the bar was silently showing a soap opera. The guy behind the bar looked like a reject from the World Wrestling Federation. He was large with a shaved head and a big, droopy moustache. He was wearing a black tee shirt with the sleeves cut off, and a Harley-Davidson logo on the front. Across his thick upper arm, just below the right shoulder, was a surprisingly neat tattoo which read *Born to Raise Hell.*

The three guys at the bar didn't appear to be listening to the music or watching the television. They weren't with each other, and maybe weren't with anyone. Ever. None of them paid any attention to the woman in the booth. I slid onto a stool next to one of them, and took out my picture of Craig Sampson.

"Ever see this guy?" I said and held the picture in front of him.

The guy was wearing a yellow rain slicker over a red plaid flannel shirt. He had a half-full beer mug in front of him and an empty shot glass beside it. He stared at the picture and back at his beer and shook his head. The bartender moved down the bar.

"What'll it be, pal?"

I held up the picture.

"Know this guy?" I said.

"We don't 'low no solicitation in here," the bartender said.

"Why not?" I said.

"Annoys the customers."

"More than the music?" I said.

"You want a drink, I'll sell you a drink," the bartender said. "Otherwise hit the road, Jack."

"'And never come back no mo' no mo'.'"

"You got that right, pal. We ain't running no fucking information booth here, you know?"

"Gee," I said, "and the place seemed so inviting."

The bartender had a white apron tied around his waist. He stared at me with his big arms folded across his chest.

"I'll have a draught beer," I said.

The bartender drew it and put it in front of me.

"Three and a quarter," he said.

"I'll run a tab," I said.

"No you won't."

I took a five from my wallet and put it on the bar. The bartender made change and slapped it down on the bar in front of me. All his motions were harsh.

I held up Sampson's picture again.

"Ever see him in here?" I said.

"Who wants to know?"

I looked carefully over each shoulder and slowly around the room, and back at the bartender.

"Must be me," I said.

"You looking for trouble?"

I grinned at him.

"If I say yes, will you tell me I've come to the right place?"

The bartender opened and closed his mouth. I knew I had stepped on his next line. I was still holding Sampson's picture up.

"Ever see him in here?" I said.

"Jesus," the bartender said, "you're a persistent bugger."

"Thanks for noticing," I said.

"And a real wiseass too."

I smiled modestly.

"What about this guy?" I said.

"Don't know him."

"Never saw him in here?"

"No."

"Ever hear of a street gang named the Death Dragons?"

"Are you some kind of cop or something?" the bartender said.

"Some kind," I said. "Ever hear of the Death Dragons?"

"No. It's not bike guys."

"No. Chinese."

"Oh, fuck, that's Chinatown shit. I don't know nothing about Chinatown."

"Ever hear of a guy named Lonnie Wu?"

"No."

"Kwan Chang?"

"Who?"

"It's a what. Kwan Chang."

He shook his head.

"How come you were so hostile when I came in?"

"I wasn't hostile, I just didn't know you."

"You're hostile to everyone you don't know?"

He looked at me as if I were disputing the law of gravity.

"Yeah," he said. "Of course."

I looked at the guys sitting along the bar.

"Any of you ever see this guy?" I said.

They shook their heads.

"Death Dragons mean anything to you? Lonnie Wu? Kwan Chang?"

They kept shaking their heads. Probably more exercise

than they were used to. I looked over at the woman in the booth.

"What's she drinking?" I said to the bartender.

"Gin, tonic, splash of grenadine."

"Jesus," I said. "Mix one up."

The bartender made the drink and set it in front of me. I paid him, picked up the drink, and walked over to the woman.

"Hi," I said and put the drink down in front of her. "Okay if I buy you a drink?"

She looked at me vaguely.

"Sure," she said.

"May I sit for a minute?"

"Sure."

I sat and took a sip of my beer and didn't say anything. She took a long pull on her drink and turned her gaze on me. The vagueness was still there, but she was focusing on me.

"Big," she said.

"I try," I said.

"I saw you back Eddie down."

"Eddie?"

"Bartender."

"I like to think it was superior charm," I said.

She shook her head.

"Naw. Eddie don't know nothing about charm. You got the look."

"The look?"

"Yeah." She drank some more pink gin and tonic. "Look says trouble."

"You've seen the look before?" I said.

"I know men. You'd break Eddie in two."

I smiled at her.

"If you asked me to."

She giggled and finished her drink. I gestured to Eddie for another one.

"You from around here?" she said.

"Boston," I said.

Eddie brought the drink around and put it in front of her. He looked at my beer. I shook my head, and he went away.

"Too good to be from Port City," she said.

She was a short, sturdy woman with thick reddish hair, and high cheekbones and a lot of bright red lipstick. Aside from the cowboy hat, she had on a too-tight horizontal-striped jersey and jeans. I couldn't tell because she was sitting down, but I'd have bet a lot that the jeans were too tight also. A long denim coat with a leather-trimmed collar hung on the corner of the booth.

"Ever see this guy?" I said and showed her my picture of Craig Sampson.

She got a pair of half glasses from her purse and put them on and took the picture from me and studied it. Then she gave it back to me and shook her head.

"No such luck," she said.

"Know a guy named Lonnie Wu?"

She drank some of her drink and lingered over the last swallow.

"God, that hits the spot, doesn't it?"

I waited.

"Lonnie Wu. Yeah, runs the Chinese restaurant up Ocean Street, near that theater."

"What do you know about him?"

"That's it," she said. "Just runs a restaurant."

"I hear he's an important man in town."

She took another appreciative swallow of her drink.

"He's Chink," she said. "How's he going to be important?"

"Good point," I said and smiled. I was oozing charm like an overripe tomato. "Know anything about the Death Dragons?"

"Who're they? Rock group?"

"Chinese street gang."

"Don't know about that. Don't know nothing about no Chinks."

She edged a little closer to me in the booth so that her thigh pressed against mine. She looked straight at me. Her eyes were big and slightly oval. But they were reddish, and puffy; and there was that unfocused look in them, as if some of the interior lights had burned out.

"Know what?" she said.

"What?"

"I like you."

"Everyone does," I said. "It's a gift."

She emptied her glass and waved at Eddie while she thought about that, and he brought her another drink.

"You like me?" she said.

"Of course," I said.

"So how come you don't talk about me? Just talk about Chinks?"

"Well, there's sort of a lot of them up here," I said.

"You got that right—what's your name?"

"Spenser."

"You got that right, Spence. There's a ka-jillion of them, and more coming."

I sipped a little beer with my left hand. She traced a forefinger on the back of my right hand where it rested on the tabletop.

"Strong," she said as if to herself.

"And more coming?" I said.

"Boat loads. Every goddamned week more Chinks come in."

"On a boat?"

She nodded.

"I live out Brant Island Road. Unload them there middle of the damn night. You married?"

"Sort of," I said.

"You got somebody?"

"Yeah."

She drank.

"Had so many somebodies can't remember their fucking names."

"Tell me about these Chinese unloading in the night?" I said.

She was singing to herself, and maybe to me, in a small, surprisingly girlish voice.

"Everybody, got somebody sometime . . ."

"I think you got the lyric wrong," I said.

"You fool around?" she said.

"No."

She nodded.

"Well, fuck you then," she said.

"Or not," I said.

"Everybody falls in love somehow . . ."

She picked up her glass and drank most of it and put it down and leaned back in the booth and closed her eyes. She began to cry with her eyes closed. I didn't say anything. Pretty soon she stopped crying and started snoring.

"Ah, Mr. Excitement," I said out loud. "You've done it again."

chapter
29

Susan and I had set up a room in Concord. The kitchen and part of the dining room were reduced to bare ruined chairs. But I had moved the refrigerator into the dining room, and the furnace worked, and there was running water. We put a bed and a table and two chairs in the front bedroom upstairs, the one with the fireplace, hung a curtain in the shower, and stocked the back bathroom with towels and other necessities. Susan and I made the bed, which wasn't as easy as it might have been, because Pearl kept getting onto it and snuggling down every time we spread something out.

"Who could ask for anything more," I said when we finally finished with the bed. "Except maybe a kitchen."

Pearl was pleased with the way we'd made the bed. She turned three circles on it, and curled herself against the plumped-up pillows which she rearranged but slightly.

"Why do we need a kitchen when we have a phone?" Susan said.

"I forgot that," I said.

It was a late Saturday afternoon, getting dark. Susan had brought a vacuum and was vacuuming fiercely. I went to the cellar, got some firewood, courtesy of the previous owner, hauled it upstairs, and built a fire. Then I went to examine the larder.

Susan had brought a picnic supper, and stashed it in a large carry-out bag in the refrigerator. I opened it fearfully. Susan was capable of an apple and two rice cakes. I looked in the bag. There were four green apples. My heart sank. But there was also cold chicken, seedless grapes, French bread, cranberry chutney, and a significant wedge of cheese. There were even paper plates and plastic utensils, and clear plastic cups. I had contributed two bottles of Krug, which lay coldly on their side in the refrigerator, and a small red and white Igloo cooler full of ice.

I carried everything upstairs and set it on the table. I opened the cooler and stuck the champagne into the ice. Susan had finished vacuuming and was aggressively dusting all surfaces.

"Isn't it better to dust before you vacuum?" I said.

"No."

I nodded and put the food on the table. Pearl immediately moved down the bed, and lay so that her nose was as close as possible to the table, without actually getting off the bed.

"Where's that blue thingie," she said as she paused in her dusting to rub a small mark off one of the window panes.

"It's not nice to call it a blue thingie," I said.

"I mean the blue tablecloth. Only a barbarian would eat off a bare tabletop."

I made sure the picnic basket was closed so Pearl would not forage in it, and went for the tablecloth. Susan went to shower. I brought the tablecloth back, put the tablecloth on the table, went to the shower and poked my head in.

"Amscray," she said.

I pulled my head out of the shower and went back to the bedroom and stood looking at the fire. My shotgun was leaning on the wall next to my place at the table, and the .9 mm Browning was neatly arranged beside the plastic knife and spoon. The Death Dragons hadn't bothered me again. But that didn't mean they wouldn't. And they probably didn't know about Concord. But that didn't mean they wouldn't, either.

We sat at the table under the low ceiling in the old house with the fire dancing in the fireplace and sipped our champagne. The cold supper lay waiting before us, and our dog was asleep on the bed.

"Amscray?" I said.

"Un huh."

"From a Harvard Ph.D.?"

"I minored in pig Latin," Susan said.

She was wearing a big white terrycloth robe that she'd brought from home, and after her shower, without makeup, her face was like a child's. Albeit a very wised-up child.

"I know just what you must have looked like," I said. "When you were a little girl."

"And I can't imagine you," she said, "as a little boy."

I smiled at her.

"Me either," I said.

We ate some chicken.

"Any progress in Port City?" she said.

"Well," I said, "I don't know if it's progress, but it's something."

I got up and went to my jacket, where it was hanging in the closet. I fished the pictures of Craig Sampson and the mystery guest and gave them to Susan. She looked at them, and then got up and went to the light and looked at them more closely. Then she came back and sat down and handed me the pictures. She had an odd, half-amused look on her face.

"I think that's Rikki Wu," Susan said.

"Why?"

Susan smiled.

"You'll like this," she said. "I was at dinner one night with Veronica Blosser and Naomi Selkirk and Rikki. Probably eight months ago. At Naomi's house. We were planning a fund-raiser for the theater."

"Sorry I missed it."

"Oh, you'd have gone crazy," Susan said. "And we were all through with the fund-raiser part and the conversation was flagging, and Naomi, who can't stand a moment's silence, said to Rikki, 'Oh darling you look so fabulous, what do you do? How do you keep looking so fabulous?' And Rikki tells us what she does."

Susan smiled again as she thought about it.

"For Rikki, looking fabulous is a full-time career: creams, unguents, potions, lotions, jellies and jams, personal trainers, massage therapists, vitamins, blah blah blah. I won't bore you with it all, but, for example, she does a series of contraction exercises to strengthen the vaginal canal."

"How strong does it have to be?" I said.

"Strong enough to keep your husband."

"Great idea," I said. "Just tighten up on him and he's yours till you relax."

"Fabulous," Susan said. "Now, here's the part that matters. She said to us, 'Girls, any man who tells you he likes hair on a woman's body is lying to you.' And Veronica says, 'Really? Do you mean *any* hair?' And Rikki says, '*Any* hair.' And Naomi looks kind of uncomfortable, which makes me think something about Naomi's situation, hirsute wise—but that's not germane. So I said to her, 'So what do you do, Rikki?' and she said, 'Electrolysis.' And we all say, 'Electrolysis? Everywhere?' and Rikki nods like a doctor confirming a diagnosis and says, 'Everywhere. My flower is like a polished pearl.' "

"Flower?"

"Flower."

"Funny, I thought I was the only one that called it that."

"I've heard what you call it," Susan said. "The electrolysis took her two years."

"She doesn't need that exercise," I said. "Two years of electrolysis would tighten up anybody's vaginal canal."

Susan carefully cut a small wedge of cheese, popped it in her mouth and chewed and swallowed.

"Yes," Susan said. "Fabulously."

"So you figure this woman with a flower like a polished pearl has got to be Rikki Wu."

"Be one hell of a coincidence," Susan said.

"Assuming it's a coincidence is not generative," I said.

"Generative," she said.

I nodded. Susan smiled.

"It's also not plausible," she said.

"Yes," I said. "Therefore, we'll assume that Craig was messing with Lonnie Wu's wife. The same Lonnie Wu who told me to get out of Port City. And tried twice to back it up."

Susan took a small bite from the upper joint of a chicken wing and put the rest of it down, and broke off a small piece of bread, and popped it in after the bite of chicken.

"Is this a clue?" Susan said, when she got through chewing.

"I think so. It's been so long since I saw one, I can't be sure."

I drank some champagne and ate some chicken and cut a wedge of apple and ate it with some cheese. Now I had a motive for Sampson's death, and the motive pointed at Lonnie Wu. It was also a perfect reason for him to want me out of town. It didn't prove anything yet, but it was, in fact, a dandy clue.

"Do you wish my flower were like a polished pearl?" Susan said.

"I'm an old-fashioned guy," I said. "I prefer the original, so to speak, unprocessed model."

"Rikki says that a man is lying if he tells you that," Susan said.

"My word is my bond," I said. "I'll be happy to back it up."

"In front of the baby?"

"She could wait in the next room," I said.

"She'll cry and scratch on the door," Susan said.

"I know the feeling," I said.

"On the other hand, if we don't put her out, she'll jump on the bed and bark."

"I know that feeling too."

We were quiet, looking at the movement of the fire against the old fire brick.

"We could abandon all hopes for ardor," Susan said.

"Un huh."

"Or you could put her in the car. She likes the car."

"Especially if I made her a chicken sandwich to take with her."

"Be sure there's no bones," Susan said.

"Then she'll feel secure and won't yowl," I said. "Can you say as much?"

Susan smiled her Adam-why-don't-you-try-this-nice-apple smile.

"I'll feel secure," she said.

chapter
30

We were heading back to Port City, four of us this time. I was driving the Mustang. Beside me was a young woman named Mei Ling, who was fluent in English, French, German, Mandarin, Cantonese, Japanese, Korean, and, for all I knew, Martian. Hawk and Vinnie were right behind us in Hawk's Jaguar.

"My father fled to Taiwan," Mei Ling was explaining to me, "ahead of the Communists. When Americans began relationships with the Communists in the early 1970s, my father feared Taiwan would fall. So he came here. My father had money. He was able to bring us all."

"You weren't born here," I said.

In preparation for Port City, Mei Ling had on a red plastic raincoat and a white kerchief over her hair. She was small-boned, with large, black eyes, and an air of precise delicacy about her.

"I was born in T'ai-pei," she said. "But I can't really remember it. My first clear memories are of growing up here. In Los Angeles, California."

"In Chinatown?"

"At first, yes, sir. Then my father bought us a house in Northridge, California."

"And now you're at Harvard."

"Yes, I'm a doctoral candidate in Asian Studies."

"Where Dr. Silverman found you."

"Yes, sir, through the student placement service. I am paying my own tuition."

"And she talked with you about this job."

"Yes, sir. She told me you are a detective who is investigating a case involving Chinese people. She said you would need a translator."

"Did she tell you that there might be some danger?"

"Yes, sir. But she said you were very good at such things and would protect me."

"I will, so will they," I said and gestured back of us at the Jaguar.

"I thought that was probably what they did, sir."

I grinned.

"And you're not scared?"

"I need the money, sir."

"Your father can't help you out?"

"He has a good business, sir. But he has six other children, and he is also the oldest son in his family and his parents are alive and he has many brothers and sisters. Besides, first he has to educate my brothers."

We turned off the highway, and started down Cabot Hill toward Chinatown. The Port City drizzle was falling randomly, and the sky was gray. There was a hard wind off the water. I could feel it push at the car.

"You know about tongs?"

She smiled at me kindly.

"All Chinese people know about tongs, sir."

"Of course, and there's no need to call me sir."

"I am comfortable calling you so," she said. "It is the way I was brought up."

"Okay," I said.

"Thank you, sir."

"You know the Kwan Chang tong?" I said.

"Yes, sir. It is the most powerful in this area."

"They run Chinatown here in Port City," I said.

"Yes, sir."

"And they use a street gang to help them," I said.

"Yes, sir. The Death Dragons."

"They teach this stuff at Harvard?" I said.

She smiled. "No need to, sir. The tongs and the street gangs they employ are part of all Chinese people's lives. They know of them even if they've never actually met anyone who's in a tong, or a street gang. They are always near us, always."

We were in Chinatown. I parked on the curb, and Hawk pulled in behind me. Hawk and Vinnie got out first, each with a shotgun. Mei Ling and I got out and stood with them in the cold wind. I turned the collar up on my leather jacket. Mei Ling stayed quite close to me, her hands deep in the pockets of her raincoat. Beside Hawk she looked nearly elfin.

"You going to be warm enough?" I said.

"Yes, sir. I have on a sweater under my raincoat."

Hawk grinned at her.

"And if you get too cold," he said, "I can put you in my pocket."

She smiled back at him.

"I am a small person," she said. "But I am quite hardy."

"Mei Ling and I will talk with people," I said. "You may as well trail along in the car and keep your powder dry."

"It always rain here?" Vinnie said.

"Yeah," I said. "Something to do with the conjunction of hills and ocean, and the prevailing winds."

"A fucking weatherman," Vinnie said to Mei Ling, and got in the car.

"I hope you'll forgive Vinnie his language," I said. "We've tried to break him out of it. But he's pretty much untrainable."

"I don't mind if people say 'fuck,' sir. Sometimes I say 'fuck' myself."

"I don't like you going in places alone," Hawk said.

"Me either, but my chances of having anyone talk to me seem better just me and Mei Ling."

"Probably are," Hawk said. "How long you be in a place, before we come in?"

I shrugged.

"Use your best judgment," I said. "If you think you should come, come in kind of quiet, so if somebody is talking you won't scare them into catatonia."

"Don't even know where that is," Hawk said. "It look funny, you send Missy running for me."

"You hear that, Missy?" I said.

"Yes, sir."

"Okay," I said. "Let's see who we can find to talk with."

"Preferably someone in a warm building, sir."

"What about the sweater?" I said.

"I should have chosen a warmer one, sir."

We walked across the sidewalk and went into a Chinese laundry.

chapter
31

No one at the laundry could tell us anything. Nor at the grocery store where mahogany-colored ducks dangled in the window, nor at the dim sum shop, nor in the tailor shop.

Back out on the street, plodding through the cold drizzle, we remained undaunted.

"Most of these Chinese people," Mei Ling said, "have never before spoken to a white person."

She was shivering. I didn't think it was so cold, but I didn't weigh ninety pounds.

"They call that speaking?" I said.

Mei Ling smiled.

"It is very Chinese to be reticent," she said. "For many centuries Chinese people got only trouble from talking. We find saying little and working hard to be a virtue."

"Novel idea," I said.

"And, of course, despite the fact that I explain to them otherwise, many of these Chinese people think you are from the government."

"And if I were?"

Mei Ling hugged herself as she walked. I could see that it was will, only, which kept her teeth from chattering.

"Then you would make them pay taxes, or find that they were here illegally and make them leave. Our history has not taught us to trust our government."

"Most histories don't," I said.

We went into a storefront painted white with large red Chinese characters on the window.

"The sign says that this is a clinic," Mei Ling said. "It is a Chinese medicine clinic."

It was warm inside the clinic. There were green plants in the window, and a big fish tank on a counter along the side. The back was draped with white sheets, which separated the examining rooms. A pleasant-looking woman in a blue pants suit with her hair in a bun came forward and said something to us. She looked at Mei Ling. Mei Ling responded, and the woman smiled and bowed slightly at me and put out her hand. I shook it.

"This is Mrs. Ong," Mei Ling said.

From somewhere behind the draped sheets a bald man in a similar blue suit joined us. Mei Ling spoke to him and he bowed and put out his hand as his wife had.

"Mr. Ong," Mei Ling said.

We shook hands. Like his wife, Ong had a warm, dry hand and a firm grip. I held out my picture of Craig Sampson.

"Have you ever seen this man?" I said.

Each took the picture and looked at it politely and smiled and looked at me and smiled. Mei Ling spoke to them. They listened to her, nodded, looked again at the picture, and spoke to Mei Ling. She answered. They said something else. Mei Ling nodded.

"They wish to take the picture in back," she said, "and study it more closely."

"Sure," I said.

Mr. and Mrs. Ong withdrew, backing away so as not to insult us with their backs.

"This mean they recognize the picture and wish to discuss what to do about it?" I said.

"I think probably," Mei Ling said. In the warm room her color had returned, and she was no longer hugging herself.

The room was lined with cupboards, each cupboard had many shelves and compartments. On top of the cupboards were glass jars containing dried things.

"That is bear gall, sir," Mei Ling said, pointing to a jar, "sea horse for kidney, grubs to clean wounds, angelica, ginseng, Yon Chiao pills, deer antlers."

"Hey," I said. "I may be a little slow on the bear gall. But I recognized the antlers. Does this stuff work?"

"What would you reply, sir, if I asked you if western medicine works."

"I would reply, 'sometimes.'"

"Yes, sir, that is what I would reply."

There was a glass case on the other side of the room. There were dried lizards in it, flattened out like stick-on wall ornaments, and short, round desiccated things in glass tubes. I asked Mei Ling.

"Those are deer legs, sir."

"For?"

Mei Ling looked at the floor.

"Male potency," she said.

"Really?"

I pretended to reach in and pocket some. Mei Ling giggled and blushed. Mr. and Mrs. Ong emerged from the backroom. Mr. Ong handed the picture back to me and shook his head. He spoke to Mei Ling.

"He says they do not know this man," Mei Ling said.

"You believe them?" I said.

"I do not know, sir. I admit that when they went in the backroom, I thought they did."

"Me too."

I looked at the both of them. Their faces were still and quiet.

"You understand any English?" I said.

They smiled politely and looked at Mei Ling. She translated. They both shook their heads, still smiling.

"They say they speak no English," Mei Ling said.

"You believe them?"

"I do not know, sir. Many Chinese people do not speak English."

"I think they recognized the picture and went out back and consulted a third party and the third party told them to be quiet."

"That is certainly possible, sir."

"You know Lonnie Wu?" I said.

Mei Ling translated. Their faces never changed. Smiling politely, they each shook their head.

"They do not know Mr. Wu," Mei Ling said.

"Of course they do," I said. "He's Kwan Chang *dai low* in Port City. He's the man in Chinatown here."

"Yes, sir."

"And, I'm wasting my time bitching about it," I said.

Mei Ling smiled at me.

"Yes, sir."

"So let's, ah, amscray."

"Excuse me, sir?"

"An expression I learned from Dr. Silverman," I said. "A form of Latin."

"Yes, sir."

As we headed for the door, I unzipped my jacket and unsnapped the safety strap on my holster. I had a pretty good guess who the third party was. If Mei Ling saw me, she gave no sign.

"Mei Ling," I said. "Let me go out first, please."

If Mei Ling wondered about that, she gave no sign. I went out first, she followed, and in the cold rain that had evolved from the drizzle, spread out, shoulder to shoulder across the sidewalk, coming toward us, were five adolescent Asian males, including my old pal Yan. I heard Mei Ling make a little gasp.

I said, "Step back in the shop, Mei Ling."

I didn't look, I was locked on Yan and company, but I could feel her move. I took the Browning from its holster, cocked it, and held it, barrel down, at my side. The group came to a halt in front of me. They all wore high-top sneakers and jeans. Most of them had baseball caps on backwards. Yan wore a purple satin finish warm-up jacket, with blue knit collar and cuffs. Nobody was showing a weapon yet, but the kid to Yan's right wore an oversized Australian outback coat unbuttoned, which might mean something bigger than a handgun. The wind had died and the rain came straight down, steady but not hard. It beaded on Yan's satin jacket. I surveyed the group which had formed a half circle on the sidewalk. No one there had reached twenty years old. Two of them were trying to grow moustaches and the results were pathetic. As opposed to the dead face that Yan had showed me when I grabbed him, his eyes were shiny, and a little nerve twitched near the corner of his mouth. All of them were excited. None of them looked uneasy.

I smiled my friendliest smile, and said, "Death Dragons, I presume."

No one spoke. No one probably understood what I said. I waited. The street was empty. The rain fell gently. The kids all watched me brightly. One of them, with the wispy moustache, spoke to Yan. Yan answered. The kid giggled. I kept my knees soft, relaxed my shoulders, took in a lot of wet air. Everything was slowing down, the way it does. The rain drops seemed to individuate. They fell big and crystalline, drifting down between us, disinterested, in no great hurry to reach the ground.

The kids were milking the moment. They were stone killers, all of them, with no capacity for pity or remorse. But they were also kids, and this was as close as their stunted lives ever brought them to play. Even the five-abreast walk up the street was something from a bad movie, as was the half circle they'd formed in front of me, and the dramatic pause that hadn't ended yet. They were having fun.

"We are kill you," Yan said.

I didn't answer. Yan was clearly in charge. He'd make the first move. I waited. The silence was so profound that I could hear the sound of the rain passing down through the air between us. The silence magnified the sound of a shotgun shell being chambered. The keys were strung tight. All five of them jumped, and turned. Hawk was there, and Vinnie Morris, behind them. Hawk to their right, Vinnie to their left. Each had a shotgun, at shoulder. It had been Hawk, who has his own sense of drama, who had waited to pump the round up when he was behind them. The kids turned back to look at me. I had the Browning up now, and aimed, straight out from the shoulder at the middle of Yan's mass.

"Maybe you aren't kill me," I said.

Again the silence. And the small rain down does fall. I knew the kids were waiting for Yan to decide. Yan looked at the Browning, steady on his chest. I could see the shine leave his eyes, like something dying.

Without taking my eyes from him, I said, "Mei Ling?"

In a moment I heard, "Yes, sir?"

"It's over. Tell them to lie facedown on the sidewalk."

Mei Ling spoke to them. Her small voice was clear and steady. The kids didn't move.

"Tell them I will count five and anyone still standing will be shot," I said.

Mei Ling spoke again. I held my left hand up, five fingers spread.

"One."

I folded over the little finger.

"Two."

The ring finger.

"Three."

They were down. They had assumed the position before. Three of them automatically clasped their hands behind their head.

"Tell them all to clasp hands behind heads, please."

Mei Ling spoke and the other two did as they were told. The excitement over, they had retreated into the speechless docility which made the rest of their life possible.

"Please ask Mr. or Mrs. Ong to call the police, Mei Ling. If they will not, you should. If there is no phone, you will need to find one."

"I have already called the police, sir. I did so when you told me to go back inside."

I took my eyes off Yan for the first time since he'd arrived, and looked down at Mei Ling. There were two smudges of color on her cheek bones, but no other sign of excitement.

"Thank you, Mei Ling."

"You're welcome, sir."

In the distance I could hear the sirens. Then a Port City patrol car wheeled into sight and pulled in beside us. The two uniforms in it got out, service pistols drawn, shielded by the car, and said, "Police, drop your weapons."

"We're the good guys," I said. "The bad guys are on the ground. Where's DeSpain?"

"He'll be along," one of the uniforms said. Both cops held position, guns leveled, as two more patrol cars pulled up, and an unmarked gray Ford behind them. The cops got out of the cars and surrounded the scene, guns drawn. DeSpain got out of the Ford, wearing a tan trenchcoat and a gray felt hat, and walked toward me, stepping squarely on Yan's back as he came. DeSpain seemed not to notice. Hawk and Vinnie lowered the shotguns. I holstered the Browning.

"Cuff the ones on the ground," DeSpain said. "Be sure and pat them down."

"What about the guys with the shotguns," one of the cops said.

"I'll take care of that end," DeSpain said. "Just clean up the gooks."

He looked at Mei Ling.

"Who's this?"

"My translator, Mei Ling Chu," I said.

DeSpain nodded.

He said, "How're you?" to Mei Ling, and looked at me.

"I gotta say, you are getting to be a royal fucking pain in the ass," DeSpain said.

"And I thought you didn't care," I said.

Behind us the wagon pulled up and the cops began to

file the five Death Dragons into it. DeSpain looked at them without emotion.

"See you can get them to headquarters before their lawyer," DeSpain said. He looked back at me.

"We need to talk," he said.

"I'll come down."

"You deliver the two shooters if I need them."

"Yes."

A patrolman was loading the Death Dragons' guns into a duffel bag. The one in the Australian coat had been carrying an Uzi.

"Okay," DeSpain said. He looked at Mei Ling and tipped his cap, and turned back to his car. Everyone left.

Hawk walked over and stood beside Mei Ling. He held the shotgun loosely at his side, barrel down to keep the rain out. He looked down at her and grinned.

"What you think of that, Missy?" he said.

"I was very scared," Mei Ling said. "I was glad when you came."

"Me too," I said.

"Saw them coming down the street," Hawk said, "and pulled around the corner. Thought we'd do better coming up behind them."

"Do you think the Ongs called someone when they went out back to study the picture?"

"Yeah," I said. "They called Lonnie Wu."

"And he sent those boys to kill you?"

"Yep."

"This is terrible business," Mei Ling said. "If I may say so, sir."

"You may and it is," I said. "I wouldn't blame you for quitting."

"No, sir, I need the money."

"And?" Hawk said.

Mei Ling looked at him for a moment. She was hugging herself again, and shivering a little. Her face was serious.

"And I know you will protect me," she said.

"Yeah," Hawk said. "We will."

"That's us," Vinnie said. "To serve and protect. Can we get in out of the fucking rain?"

"Yes," Mei Ling said. "I would like that too."

chapter
32

"I have something I want you to hear," Susan said.

I came from her kitchen into her living room, upstairs from her office. Susan's last patient had finished his fifty minutes. The early winter darkness had settled against the windows. There was a fire in her fireplace, courtesy of me, which was the only time a fire ever happened there. Pearl had been fed and was asleep on the floor in front of the fire. A Brunswick stew simmered in Susan's kitchen, courtesy of me, which was the only time a Brunswick stew ever happened there. I was drinking a bottle of Rolling Rock. Susan had some red wine.

"Listen," Susan said, and pressed the playback button on her answering machine.

A voice said, "Dr. Silverman, this is Angela Trickett . . ."

Susan said, "Nope," and hit the fast forward. She let it run for a moment and hit it again.

A voice said, "Susan, it's Gwenn . . ."

"Nope." Fast forward. "This next one is it."

"Dr. Silverman. This will be hard to hear, maybe, but you need to know. Your boyfriend is not faithful to you. I know this from personal experience, which I regret. But you have the right to know. I am not the first one."

There was a pause, then the sound of the phone hanging up. Susan hit the stop button and looked at me.

I looked sheepishly at her.

"That damned Madonna," I said. "Can't keep her mouth shut."

Susan smiled.

"I thought I recognized the voice."

"Play it again," I said.

Susan did. We listened.

"Again," I said.

We listened.

"Jocelyn Colby," I said.

"My God," Susan said, "I think you're right."

"I'm right," I said.

"Then there's something else. She has called me two or three times asking if you were there, saying that she'd expected to see you, but you weren't where you were supposed to be."

"What the hell does that mean?" I said.

"Well, first of all, I'm assuming that you've not been balling Jocelyn Colby."

"This is true," I said.

"So she's lying to make me think you're unfaithful. Calling me up looking for you was probably a way of planting suspicion. 'Well, where is he?' I was supposed to say to myself. In fact, since you are often irregular in

your hours, I never thought anything about it, and since
she had no message for you, I never bothered to say
anything."

"She ever speak to you direct?"

"No, always on the machine. I assume she called
during office hours, knowing I wouldn't pick up."

My beer was gone. I went to the kitchen and opened
another bottle, looked at my stew, poured a little of the
beer into it, gave it a stir, and went back into the living
room. Susan was sitting on the couch with her shoes off
and her feet tucked under her. She held her wine glass in
both hands and stared over the rim of it into the fire. I sat
beside her on the couch.

"So why is she doing this?" Susan said.

"Last time I saw her she was mad at me, because I told
her no one was following her."

"And?"

"And she called me a prick master."

"Prick master? What a dandy phrase. But I meant 'and
what resulted from the fact that you said no one was
following her?'"

"I was going to stop being her shadow."

"Do you think she knew that no one was following
her?"

"Unless she's delusional," I said. "There was no one
there."

"So why would she tell you she was being followed?"

"To get my attention?"

"And eventually your companionship."

Pearl shifted on the floor and made a snurffing sound
in her sleep. I drank a little of my beer.

"Just before she was calling me a prick master she was
complaining that I was going to spend time with you."

Susan nodded. We were quiet. The flames moved in

the fireplace. A bubble of residual moisture, squeezed by the heat, oozed out of the end of one log and vaporized with a barely audible hiss.

"Is this a case of 'hunk city' strikes again?" I said.

"She's jealous," Susan said. "She has attached to you in some way, and she's jealous of me."

"Well, any woman would be," I said.

Susan went on as if I hadn't spoken. When she began to think about something, she could think it to a crisp.

"You are a powerful man—in a protector, rescuer, kind of way."

"She talked about being rescued."

"It's a voguish pop psyche jargon phrase at the moment," Susan said. "I hear it in therapy all the time. And it's a useful concept, as long as everyone understands that it is shorthand for a much larger and more complicated emotional issue."

"Does she seriously think she can break us apart by anonymous accusations of infidelity?" I said.

Susan smiled.

"Fancy talk for a guy with an eighteen-inch neck," she said.

"I been bopping a shrink," I said.

"Lucky you," Susan said. "A woman like that reflects her own emotional life. She has no depth of commitment; she doesn't understand it in others. She has no trust; she assumes others don't either. If he doesn't want me, it's because there's someone else; if I can get rid of someone else, he'll want me. It's an adolescent vision of love, which is to say romanticized sexual desire."

"Thank you, doctor."

"Be sure you understand it. I'll be passing out blue books before supper."

"You have any thoughts on what I should do about this?"

"Ignore it," Susan said.

"You think she'll keep calling?"

"Probably, but only on my machine. She won't want to talk with me."

"You shouldn't have to be bothered."

"No bother," Susan said. "Just another message on my machine at night. It might get exciting. She might give me details on what you and she do."

"She's pretty good-looking," I said.

"Un huh."

"Maybe, just to help her regain her mental health, if I came across for her?"

"Or maybe the disappointment would put her over the edge," Susan said.

"You never seem disappointed," I said.

"I'm a Harvard graduate," Susan said.

"Yeah, good point. I guess we'd better not risk it with Jocelyn."

"I agree," Susan said.

"Another thing about her," I said. "She says she and Christopholous are, or were, lovers, that whoever was following Christopholous was probably jealous of his love for her, or hers for him, she wasn't clear about that."

"Really," Susan said. "I didn't know about that."

"Apparently Christopholous didn't either," I said. "He was puzzled at the suggestion."

"What did he say when you quoted Jocelyn?"

"I didn't. I'm trying not to say more than I need to say in this deal. At least until I get some idea of what I'm talking about."

"That seems prudent," Susan said.

"I don't think Christopholous was lying," I said. "Why

would he? There's no reason he shouldn't date Jocelyn. He's divorced. She's divorced."

"She's widowed," Susan said, "not that it makes any difference, I guess."

"She told me she was divorced."

Susan widened her eyes.

"Really," she said. "She told me she was widowed."

"You know any details? Husband's name? Where they were married? How he died?"

Susan shook her head. One of the logs settled in the fireplace. The momentary flare brightened Susan's face, and threw a shadow that made her eyes seem even bigger than they were.

"No. Just that he died 'tragically' before she joined the company."

I leaned back a little and stretched my legs out toward the fire and put my arm around Susan's shoulder.

"Jocelyn appears to lie," I said.

"True," Susan said.

On the floor Pearl opened her eyes and stared at me with my arm around Susan. She thought about that for a moment, then, seemingly from the prone position, jumped up on the couch and insinuated herself vigorously between us.

"Pearl appears to be jealous."

"Also true," Susan said.

Pearl leaned into Susan in such a way as to get most of my arm off of Susan and around Pearl. I looked at her. She lapped me on the nose.

"As a mental health professional," I said, "do you have a view on Jocelyn?"

"I think she might be nuts," Susan said.

"Could you put that in terms a layman can understand?"

"Well, she seems to have some unresolved conflicts which center on men, particularly men in positions of power or authority, or perhaps merely older men."

"Is it too early to suggest that she might have some sort of problem with her father?"

Susan smiled at me.

"Yes," she said. "It is too early."

Half sitting, half sprawled between us, Pearl shifted her weight from me onto Susan.

"Is it too early to suggest that Pearl has unresolved issues about being a Canine American Princess?"

"No. I think we have empirical support for that diagnosis," Susan said. Pearl lapped Susan's ear. Susan turned her head, trying to escape. Pearl persisted. "Though perhaps it is not an unresolved issue."

We sat quietly for a while.

"Maybe she was following Christopholous," I said.

"You think?"

"One of the things stalkers get out of stalking is a sense of power over the person they are stalking."

Susan nodded.

"And, thinking of it in this light, it was an odd remark, that the stalker was stalking Christopholous because the stalker was jealous."

"Unless it was true," Susan said.

"And she were the stalker," I said.

"She forms an obsessive attachment to Jimmy, because he's older and he's the head of her acting company, and she tends to form such attachments," Susan said.

She was staring into the fire. Her wine glass was still nearly full in her hands. I knew she'd forgotten about it as she tracked her hypothesis.

"And he doesn't reciprocate. She assumes there's another woman, and trails him to see if there is."

"And maybe," I said, "because it makes her feel good to trail him."

"Yes."

"And then I come along and, being entirely irresistible, as you well know, replace Christopholous in her affections."

"And she tells you she's being followed so you'll pay attention to her."

"If we're right," I said, "this is not a healthy woman."

"No, she must be very unhappy."

"So maybe I've got the stalker," I said.

"Maybe. So who killed Craig?"

"I have no idea," I said.

Susan leaned over and kissed me on the mouth.

"But you will," she said. "What's for supper?"

"Brunswick stew, French bread, tomato chutney," I said.

"Shall we eat some?"

"That was part of my plan," I said.

"What was the rest?"

"Well," I said. "If I can't help Jocelyn out . . ."

Susan smiled at me.

"The last boy scout," she said.

chapter
33

We were in my office. Vinnie was listening to doo wop
on his head phones, Hawk was still reading Cornel West,
and I sat at my desk looking at Craig Sampson's FBI file.
When I got through, I passed it over to Hawk. He
dog-eared the page in his book and put it on the corner of
my desk and took the file and read it. When he was
through, he passed it back.

"Where you say the Chinese broad from?" Hawk said.

"Rikki Wu? T'ai-pei."

Hawk nodded and picked up his book again. I sat and
stared at the file folder. Vinnie was bobbing his head to
the music only he could hear. Behind me the window
rattled. I swiveled my chair and, for a change of pace,
stared out the window for a while. It was bright outside,
and very warm for November, but the wind was strong.
Where I could see the sky between the buildings, it was

a weak blue, and the off-white clouds were tattered-looking as they trailed east toward the harbor.

According to the file that Lee Farrell had dropped off, Craig Sampson would be forty-one were he still alive. He had enlisted in the army, in August of 1971, had basic training at Ft. Dix, gone to the army language school at Monterey, and spent a year and a half with a Military Assistance Group in Taiwan. He had the rank of Specialist 3rd class when he was honorably discharged in July 1974.

From somewhere I heard a siren. Police Headquarters was up Berkeley Street a couple of blocks, and beyond that, facing onto Columbus, was a firestation. Sirens were the sound of the city; urban be-bop.

I swiveled my chair back around. Hawk looked up, dog-eared his book again, and put his feet up on the corner of my desk. His cowboy boots were gleaming with polish.

"Everywhere we look," Hawk said, "there's a god-damned Chinaman."

"I don't think we're supposed to call them that," I said.

"Okay, how 'bout 'a Asian gentleman.'"

"I think you need to get the phrase 'Pacific Rim' in there somewhere," I said.

"Lemme practice," Hawk said, "I know I can get it right."

"Okay," I said. "For the moment, anyway, everywhere we look there's a goddamned Chinaman."

"What we know is Rikki Wu from Taiwan. Craig Sampson stationed in Taiwan. Rikki Wu pretty surely bopping Craig Sampson. Rikki Wu's husband's Kwan Chang's man in Port City. He tell you to buzz off. You don't and various people from the Pacific Rim trying to blow your brains out. You know where Lonnie Wu is from?"

"No."

"You figure maybe Craig been buzzing Rikki longer than we thought?"

"Maybe."

"You figure DeSpain know that and tell you there's no record on Sampson so you won't follow it up?"

"Maybe. Or maybe he just went to Triple I and it wasn't there, so he didn't go further."

"Like he don't know that there can be clerical errors," Hawk said. "You know DeSpain, you think he that sloppy in a homicide?"

"No."

"And they toss Sampson's room," Hawk said. "And they don't find the nude pictures under the bed that a fucking girl scout would find in ten minutes."

"I know," I said. "That's been bothering me too."

Vinnie took one tape out of his Walkman and put in another. He evinced no interest in our conversation.

"So you got a theory?" Hawk said.

"About the pictures, yeah. I figure Port City didn't really search Sampson's room. They just went in and emptied a few drawers and made a mess so that it would look like they searched it. Probably took them five minutes."

"Which explains why they made such a mess," Hawk said.

"Un huh. Of course DeSpain could have sent a couple guys over and they didn't want to bother," I said.

"And DeSpain didn't know they fucking off on him," Hawk said.

"Yeah."

"You think DeSpain's people fuck off on him and he don't know it?"

"No and no," I said.

"So?"

"DeSpain's covering up," I said.

"And one of the things he covering up is Wu's connection to Sampson."

"Yes."

"You know why?"

"No."

"You see any connection with the stalker?"

"No, but I think I've got that one figured out."

I told him about Jocelyn and the phone calls.

"She *is* neurotic," Hawk said. "Be obsessed with you, when I on the scene?"

"Before me she was obsessed with Christopholous," I said. "If we're right."

Hawk shook his head.

"Must be a honkie thing," he said. "You figure Lonnie had Sampson killed?"

"Possibility," I said. "Found out he was taking nude pictures of Rikki's flower and sent somebody to pop him on stage so Rikki'd be sure to notice."

"So," Hawk said. "You got a pretty good idea about the stalker. You got a pretty good idea on who killed Sampson. Why don't we declare everything solved and get the hell out of there?"

"I don't think so," I said.

"'Cause you like hanging around with me and Vinnie every day."

I shrugged.

"It's all theory," I said. "We got no case against Lonnie. Even if we turn what I know over to DeSpain, is he going to follow it up?"

"Not likely," Hawk said.

"We don't know Jocelyn was following Christopholous."

"We know," Hawk said. "We just can't prove it."

"Same thing."

"Not in my world," Hawk said.

"Yeah, but we're working in mine."

"Which do make it tiresome," Hawk said. "We working in mine, we solve this problem a lot quicker."

"I know, but even if we did it your way, there's
something wrong in Port City. We remove Lonnie Wu,
say, ah, surgically, Kwan Chang will have another *dai
low* in place the next day."

"Gonna happen however Lonnie's removed," Hawk
said.

"I know," I said.

"So what's the difference?"

"A real police department can sort of counterweight
the tong," I said. "I gotta know about DeSpain."

Hawk grinned.

"And?" he said.

I shrugged. "And I told Susan I'd clean it up."

"Un huh," Hawk said.

Both of us grinned.

We had known each other for a very long time.

chapter
34

I sat in DeSpain's office and asked him about the Death
Dragons he'd arrested.

"Out," he said.

"Already?"

"Yeah. Lawyer was here when we brought them in.
What the hell were they guilty of, anyway? Just walking
along the street when you people braced 'em."

"They have permits for the weapons they were carrying?" I said.

DeSpain grinned without meaning anything by it.

"You got anything new on the Sampson killing?" I
said.

"Nope."

"I've come up with a few pieces of this and that," I
said.

DeSpain leaned back in his chair and clasped his hands behind his head.

"And you're going to tell me," he said.

"Yeah."

And I did. I told him what I knew and what I supposed. I told him about Rikki Wu, and the pictures, and about Craig Sampson and his military career, and about Jocelyn and her imaginary stalker. DeSpain folded his thick arms across his chest, tilted his chair back, and sat motionless while I talked. The hard light from the fluorescent ceiling fixture washed out his features and made him look haggard. Probably did the same thing to me. When I finished, DeSpain didn't move. His expression didn't change.

"So?" he said.

"What's going on up here," I said.

DeSpain didn't speak. He simply sat.

"I called a state cop I worked with once," I said. "Guy named Healy, you know him?"

DeSpain was impassive.

"Head of Criminal Investigation Division, now. He knows you. Says you were a hell of a cop. Played it pretty close to the outer edge sometimes, but a hell of a cop. Said you had a big future with the Staties. Said if you stayed, you'd be head of CID, instead of him."

"I know Healy," DeSpain said.

"So how come you didn't get Sampson's prints?"

DeSpain shrugged.

"Maybe Triple I screwed up. Clerks make mistakes. But I found out Sampson was in the army without asking."

DeSpain stared directly at me. His eyes were without expression.

"I found the pictures in ten minutes."

"So?"

"So you're covering up."

The lines around DeSpain's mouth got deeper.

"You could get in bad trouble talking like that."

"I could get in bad trouble eating shellfish in the Happy Haddock," I said.

"Yeah."

DeSpain wheeled his chair around and sat with his back to me staring out the window at the slate gray morning.

"No point trying to scare you off," he said. "I know about you. Hasn't worked for Lonnie."

He put one foot up on the windowsill and leaned further back in his chair. Outside his window the Port City Police Department had parked their cars in orderly rows, where the monotonous rain washed them bright.

"Still I'm the Chief of Police here. I got quite a lot of push, I really have to use it."

"How come you left the state police?" I said.

"Chief in a small city like this one, sort of out by itself, if he's any good, can get a lot of control," DeSpain said.

"How come you're not trying to find out who killed Sampson?" I said.

"Starts by getting the chain of command in good working order, sifting out the discipline problems."

"You in Wu's pocket?" I said.

"One thing you do is you make sure everything is hunky-dory up on the hill, streets are safe. Keep the Portagies and Slants out of the good neighborhoods."

"You connected to Sampson? Jocelyn Colby? Rikki Wu?"

"You keep the living easy up on the hill, you can do most of what you want down here." DeSpain's voice was a soft, flat rumble. He turned his chair slowly back toward me with an easy shove of his foot on the windowsill. He looked at me, his eyes as lifeless as ball bearings.

"You can do what you want down here."

I waited. DeSpain waited. The rain drizzled on the neat row of black-and-whites in the lot.

"You got nothing to say to me?" I said.

"You got a chance now," DeSpain said, "to walk away. Take it. Walk. You keep following these tracks and you'll walk into a big nasty thing that'll eat you whole."

The silence in the office was heavy. DeSpain and I looking at each other and not speaking. Finally I stood up.

"That's who I am, DeSpain. I'm a guy who follows tracks."

"I know," DeSpain said. "I know."

chapter
35

We were in Hawk's car. Mei Ling was in front with him. I got in the back with Vinnie. Hawk looked at me in the mirror.

"DeSpain throw himself on your mercy?"

"And begged forgiveness," I said.

"Tole you it was a waste of time," Hawk said.

Mei Ling half turned in the front seat. She had on her slicker again and a slightly too big New York Yankees baseball cap, with an adjustable plastic strap in the rear. She had fed her black hair through the strap opening. It formed a flowing pony tail along her back. Under the large bill of the cap her black eyes looked too big for her face.

"You suspect the Police Chief, sir?"

"Yes, I do."

She smiled.

"Why is that funny, Mei Ling?"

"You are learning what Chinese people have always known. It is better not to trust the authorities. It is better to have a tong to trust."

"The tong is who sent the Death Dragons when we were in Chinatown," I said.

"That is true also, sir. Chinese people do not believe life is easy."

"Chinese people got that right," I said.

"What now?" Vinnie said. Vinnie was never one for small talk.

"I figure Jocelyn Colby is the sissy in this deal. We may as well go yell at her. Maybe she'll break down and tell us something."

"Be a nice change," Hawk said.

Mei Ling smiled at him when he spoke.

"She should be at the theater, this time of day," I said.

Vinnie shook his head.

"Been playing cops and robbers all my life," he said. "First time I been a cop."

Hawk pulled the Jaguar away from the curb and we headed for the theater.

"What do you know about Chinese immigration?" I said to Mei Ling.

Hawk glanced at me in the rearview mirror.

"I heard something in a bar the other day," I said.

Mei Ling tucked her feet up on the front seat. I could see her gathering herself to explain.

"In the nineteenth century," she said, "Chinese people came here, did any work, for any wage. This seemed to make people scornful of them, and afraid of them taking jobs from *low faan*." Mei Ling smiled at me and dipped her head in apology.

"Ain't that always the way," Hawk said.

Beside me, Vinnie sat quietly, his shotgun leaning against his left thigh, his eyes moving over the street scene as we drove. He had his earphones in place again, grooving on Little Anthony and the Imperials.

"So," Mei Ling said, "the U.S. Congress passed the Chinese Exclusion Act in 1882, which said that no Chinese laborers or their wives could come here. And it excluded Chinese people who were here already from most jobs."

I nodded. I was actually looking for more current information, but Mei Ling was liking her recitation so much I didn't have the heart to interrupt.

"When World War Two came, and the United States was allied with China against the Japanese, the Exclusion Act was repealed, and in 1982 after United States recognition, the People's Republic of China was granted an immigration quota in line with the Immigration Act of 1965."

"Which meant?"

"Twenty thousand Chinese people a year were permitted to come to the United States."

Mei Ling looked at Hawk. He grinned at her.

"You know a lot of stuff, Missy," he said and turned onto Ocean Street toward the Port City Theater.

"What about the rest?" I said.

"Illegal immigrants?"

"Yeah."

"There are many. Maybe most. They pay a very large amount of money to come here. Thirty, forty, fifty thousand U.S. dollars," Mei Ling said. "For this they are delivered to America, often to an employment agent who gets them a job, and they disappear into Chinatown."

"Where do they get the money?" I said.

"They borrow it from the alien smuggler, or the

employment agent, or the ultimate employer, and they pay it off out of their wages."

"Which are low," I said.

"Yes."

"Often below minimum," I said, "because they are illegal immigrants, they can't complain, they speak no English, and they can't quit because they owe their soul to the company store."

"I don't understand 'the company store,'" Mei Ling said.

"It's from a song," Hawk said. "They can't leave because their wages are owed. Sort of like slavery."

"I see. Yes."

We parked on a hydrant in front of the theater.

"You know any illegal immigrants?" I said.

Mei Ling hesitated, and looked once at Hawk, before she answered.

"Yes."

"I'd like to meet one," I said.

Again Mei Ling looked momentarily at Hawk.

"Of course," she said.

I left her with Hawk and Vinnie and went into the theater. As I crossed the sidewalk I felt exposed, like some sort of quarry in an open field. The longer I stayed in Port City, the more I had that feeling. I was aware of the comforting weight of the Browning automatic on my right hip. The front windows of the theater were filled with posters advertising a season of Shakespeare's history plays. I could follow most of those. I would even enjoy several of them.

Jocelyn wasn't at rehearsal. Lou Montana was clearly annoyed about that, and about me asking for her. Everyone else in Port City wanted to kill me; simple annoyance was a relief. I went to the lobby and called

Jocelyn Colby's home at a pay phone. I got her machine.

"This is Jocelyn. I'm dying to talk to you, so leave your name and number and a brief message if you want to, and I'll call you right back as soon as I get home. Have a nice day."

I hung up and went upstairs to Christopholous' office. I'd have a nice day later. He was in there reading a book on the Elizabethan age by E. M. W. Tillyard. He put the book, still open, facedown on his desk when I came in.

"You wouldn't happen to know where Jocelyn Colby is?" I said.

"Jocelyn? I assume she's in rehearsal."

"Nope."

"Did you ask Lou?"

"Yeah."

"I suppose he was angry that you interrupted his rehearsal."

"He was, but I've recovered from it," I said.

"I imagine you have," Christopholous said.

"I know I've asked you before, but you're sure there was no romantic connection between you and Jocelyn?"

Christopholous smiled wearily.

"I'm sure," he said. "We were friends. Jocelyn's very engaging. She'd come in and have coffee with me sometimes and we'd talk. But there was no romance."

"Maybe on her part?"

"You flatter me," Christopholous said. "An over-weight, aging Greek?"

I shrugged.

"Chacun à son goût," I said. "Do you happen to remember how Craig Sampson came to join the theater company?"

Christopholous blinked.

"Craig?" he said.

"The late Craig," I said.

"I . . . I suppose he, ah, he simply applied and auditioned and was accepted."

"Was he a gifted actor?" I said.

"Well, you saw him, what do you think?"

"Surely you jest," I said. "That play would swallow the Barrymores."

"Yes, quite true. Craig was competent, I think, not gifted."

"Anybody use any influence on his behalf?"

"Influence?"

"Influence."

"This is not some political hack patronage operation," Christopholous said.

"Do you make a profit on ticket sales?"

"Of course not, no genuinely artistic endeavor makes a profit on its work."

"So how do you make up the difference?"

"You're suggesting I barter jobs for donations?"

"I'm asking if an influential contributor asked you to take a look at Sampson."

"People are often brought to our attention. Doesn't mean we hire them."

"Who brought Sampson to your attention?"

Christopholous looked ragged, as if his genial composure was starting to fray.

"I didn't say anyone brought him to our attention."

I waited.

"I do think, and I can't remember every personnel decision we make here, but I do think it might have been Rikki Wu who sent Craig's head shot and résumé along."

"I think it was too," I said. "It might have been useful had you mentioned their connection earlier."

"Rikki is a friend," Christopholous said. "And a

generous patron. I saw no reason to involve her in a criminal investigation."

"Did you know they had a relationship?" I said.

"A relationship? You mean an intimate relationship? You do, don't you? That's ridiculous."

"Yeah, it is," I said. "But it probably got Craig Sampson killed."

chapter
36

"We are going to a *gong si fong,*" Mei Ling said.

It was early evening. We were in Hawk's Jaguar, in Boston, parked on Harrison Ave down back of the Tufts Medical Center, mid Chinatown, outside of a large red brick city housing project.

"Chinese lady has a rent-controlled apartment, and she has turned it into a place for bachelors. It is, of course, illegal," Mei Ling said.

"I'm shocked," I said.

"My cousin lives here with nine other men. Everyone else here is a waiter, they have gone to work. I have promised him you will not tell anyone."

"Promise," I said.

"Any good takeout around here, Mei Ling?" Vinnie said.

"I don't know," she said. "I have never come here to eat."

"Place on the corner looks all right," Vinnie said. "Chicken with cashews?"

Hawk nodded. He looked at Mei Ling. She smiled.

"We be here, Missy," he said.

Mei Ling nodded and got out with me. Vinnie got out too, and we headed toward the Bo Shin restaurant on the corner of Kneeland. We went into the apartment building. The *gong si fong* was on the third floor. There was no elevator.

"Many Chinese men who come here cannot afford to bring their wives," Mei Ling said, as we walked up the stairs, "especially the illegal ones."

"Your cousin illegal?"

"Yes, sir. They come here, live as cheaply as they can, pay off the smugglers, send money home, and save up to open a business and bring their family."

The building had all the usual public housing charm. No expense had been spared on cinder block and linoleum and wire mesh over the ceiling fixtures. We knocked on a blank door with no number, and a slight Chinese man in a white shirt and black pants opened the door and smiled at us and bowed. Mei Ling spoke to him in Chinese.

"My cousin's name is Liang," Mei Ling said to me.

Liang bowed again and put his hand out.

"How do you do?" he said.

I shook his hand. He backed away from the door and gestured us in. For a minute I was disoriented. The entry door led almost at once to a blank plywood wall. A hallway ran right and left, parallel to the outside corridor, punctuated with plywood doors, padlocked shut. The only light came from the bare bulb in a wall sconce at the far end. Liang led us along the plywood hallway to the last door and into his room. It was so narrow I could have touched both walls with my fingertips. It was maybe seven feet long and was filled almost entirely with a pair of bunk beds, one above the other. There were two suitcases under the bed, and several shirts and pants on hangers flat against the wall. Light came from one of those portable construction lights with spring clamps attached to the head frame of the bunks. I had seen better-looking graves.

"How much you pay for this?" I said.

Liang looked at Mei Ling. She translated. He answered.

"Liang pays one hundred dollars a month," she said. "So does the other man." She nodded at the top bunk.

"And there's four other cubicles like this?" I said.

Mei Ling translated. Liang nodded.

"Rent-controlled, the place costs the landlord maybe two, two fifty a month," I said more to myself than to Mei Ling. There were no surprises here for Mei Ling. "Gives her seven fifty, eight hundred a month profit."

Liang spoke to Mei Ling.

"He wants to show us the rest," Mei Ling said and we followed him along the hall to the kitchen. There was an ancient gas refrigerator in there, and a gas stove, and a darkly stained porcelain sink. The faucet dripped into the sink. The refrigerator didn't work. The stove did, but there was no evidence that anyone used it. Past the kitchen was a toilet with no seat, and a showerstall with no curtain.

"He got a job?" I said to Mei Ling.

"Yes. He sells fruits and vegetables," she said. "From a stand. He could afford to live better, but he doesn't choose to. He chooses to save his money."

She spoke to Liang. He answered with a lot of animation.

"He earned $31,000 last year, and saved $25,000. He pays no taxes. He has already paid off the smuggling fee. Next year he says he will bring his wife from China."

"Ask him how he got here," I said.

Mei Ling talked. Liang looked at me covertly as she spoke. He answered her. She shook her head. Spoke again. Liang nodded and spoke for several minutes.

"Liang is from Fujian Province," Mei Ling said. "He saw the local official, who arranges such things. He sent Liang to Hong Kong, and then to Bangkok. From Bangkok, Liang flew to Nicaragua. He went in a truck to Vera Cruz, Mexico, and went on a boat to the United States."

"Where'd he land?" I said.

"Liang was brought ashore in a small boat at night in Port City. He stayed there for a week and then came to Boston. The trip took him three months."

We were standing in the dismal kitchen, with the steady drip of the leaky faucet the only sound other than our voices. Several cockroaches scuttled across the one countertop and disappeared behind the stove. I looked at Liang. He smiled politely.

"Three months," I said.

"Some it takes much longer," Mei Ling said. "They have to stop each place and work. Some have to smuggle narcotics, or go back and smuggle others in to pay for their passage. If there are women, they often have to be prostitutes to pay."

"Does he know the name of the man in Port City in charge of the smuggling?"

She spoke to Liang. Liang shook his head.

"He says he doesn't," Mei Ling said.

"You believe him?"

"I don't know," Mei Ling said. "But I know he will not tell you."

"Lonnie Wu?" I said.

Liang looked blank.

"Of course it is," I said. "We all know it. But even if Liang would tell me it was, he wouldn't say so in court."

"Yes, sir," Mei Ling said. "That is true."

I looked around me.

"This was originally a studio apartment," I said. "Now ten men live here."

"Yes, sir."

I shook my head. I wanted to say something about how this wasn't the way it should be. But I knew too much and had lived too long to start talking now about "should."

"Send me your huddled masses," I said. "Yearning to breathe free."

chapter
37

Most of the people who came to Brant Island, north of
Port City, did so in the daytime, and came to watch birds.
They crossed the narrow causeway in the sunshine and
went to the rustic gazebo with their binoculars and
waited to catch sight of a bird they'd never seen before.

It was deep black when we came. And cold. Vinnie
stayed with the car, parked out of sight off the road
behind some scrub white pines and beach plum bushes.
Hawk and I walked to the island with Mei Ling between
us. There was no moon. The island was only about a
hundred feet from shore, but the steady wash of the
ocean against the causeway and the cold press of the
darkness made it seem remote. It was our fourth night of
watching, and the first in which there was no moon. We
reached the little gazebo. It offered a vantage point but
very little in protection from the cold wind off the water.

Hawk leaned against one of the columns that held the gazebo's roof up, and Mei Ling stood very close to him, her hands pushed as deep as she could get them into the pockets of her down coat. I began to look at the ocean through a night scope.

"How can he see?" Mei Ling said to Hawk.

"Off a nine-volt alkaline battery in the handle," Hawk said. I glanced at him. Like that explained it. He grinned. And Mei Ling looked at him as if now she understood. I went back to looking at the ocean. The sea sound was loud where I stood. But in the surreal circular imagery of the scope, the waves moved silently. If they came once a month and this was our fourth night, our chances were about one in seven. Maybe better since there was no moon.

"What does he expect to learn here?" Mei Ling said.

She didn't address me directly because in her view I was busy, and shouldn't be interrupted. The result was that she talked about me as if I weren't there.

"Won't know," Hawk said, "till we see it."

"But to come out here every night and watch the ocean. They might not come for weeks."

"They might not," Hawk said.

"They might have showed up the first night," I said.

The surface of the water was never still, alternately engorged and prolapsed, smoothing, ruffling, cresting as it came to shore, until the waves fragmented on the rocks, and yet always waves forming and coming on, always changing, always the same. . . . Maybe two hundred yards out on the dark ocean, dark against the dark sky, was the opaque silhouette of a ship. There was no arrival. It simply appeared in the lens and sat motionless. I took the scope down and handed it to Hawk.

"On the horizon," I said, "about one o'clock."

Hawk looked, swept the scope slowly along the horizon and stopped and made a small adjustment and held.

"Yessiree bob," he said in a flat, midwestern twang. Hawk could sound like anyone he wanted to. He handed the scope to Mei Ling.

"On the horizon," he said. "Around where one o'clock would be if it were a clock face."

Mei Ling looked. It took her a minute, but she found it. She seemed thrilled.

"Doesn't have to be smuggling immigrants," I said.

"No, it doesn't," Hawk said.

We waited in the darkness and the wind and the cold with the waves moving below us. We took turns looking through the glass, and then, finally, we heard the soft thump of an engine. We couldn't find it until it was close and then we picked it up. It was a wide flat launch open to the elements with the engine housing in the middle of the boat. Crowded tight into it were people. The engine thump was the only sound the boat made. The people were silent. The boat bumped in close to the rocks, so close that I could see the buffer bags that the crew tossed over to fend off the rocks. The boat motor kept running, and the boat stayed headed in against the jumble of granite that helped form the breakwater below us. The people scrambled off, most of them carrying nothing, a few carrying small suitcases or paper bags, or small bundles. It looked dangerous.

We stayed motionless in the gazebo, watching the dark figures in the night, only a few yards away. They were barely visible. No one spoke. They moved in a single file along the rocks and up onto the causeway. Someone led them across the causeway. There might have been a hundred of them. When the last of them scrambled up the rocks, the launch backed away and moved slowly parallel to the shore, south around the point opposite Brant Island and out of sight. I looked through the scope at the horizon. The ship was gone. I glanced at the causeway. The people were gone. The cove below Brant Island was empty and soundless except for the ocean, which was ceaseless.

All of us were quiet as if in the aftermath of a somber ritual we neither sought nor understood. The ghostly procession drifting soundless and phantasmagoric through the near-lightless night seemed more than merely illegal immigrants, though surely they were that. There was something antediluvian in the spectral progress from the sea to the shore and into the darkness that all three of us must have felt though none of us spoke of it.

"The last boat from Xanadu," I said.

chapter
38

When I went through my office mail I always made a pile of mail that I intended to open, a pile of the bills to be paid on the thirtieth of the month, and threw away the junk mail unopened. There was always a lot of junk mail. There was a package wrapped in brown paper, with no return address on it. It had been addressed in green ink, and been mailed in Boston two days prior. I put it in the mail-to-be-opened pile.

Vinnie and Hawk were there. Vinnie was cleaning his shotgun.

"Fucking barrel's going to rust through, we don't stop going to Port City," Vinnie said. Hawk was reading his book. He nodded without taking his eyes from the page.

"What's the name of the book," Vinnie said. He wasn't wearing his Walkman and he was restless.

"On Race," Hawk said.

"Yeah. How come you reading that?"

"The brother's a smart man," Hawk said.

"That racial shit bother you?" Vinnie said.

I was done with the throw-away mail and turned to the package. The envelopes that might have checks, I saved for last.

"You got a problem with me being black, Vinnie?"

"No."

"Me either. So at the moment I got no racial shit to be bothered by, you know? I try to work on that level."

I opened the package. It was a videotape cassette. It was labeled "Jocelyn Colby." I turned it over. There was nothing else. I didn't have a videotape player.

"Either of you got a VCR?" I said.

Hawk shook his head. "Already seen 'Debbie Does Dallas,'" he said.

"I had one," Vinnie said. "Old lady took it with her when she split."

Hawk said, "Didn't know you was married, Vinnie."

Vinnie grinned.

"I didn't either," he said. "Probably why she split."

I picked up the phone and called Susan.

"I have a video tape that I would like to view on your machine," I said when she answered. "If I brought an elegant lunch, perhaps you'd like to take a break from healing the loony and watch it with me."

"It's not one of those disgusting porn thingies, is it?"

"I don't know, it came in the mail and it says Jocelyn Colby on it."

"I have a two-hour break," Susan said. "One to three."

"You disappointed it's not a disgusting porn thingie?" I said.

"Yes," she said and hung up.

Hawk and Vinnie dropped me off and waited out front.

I went in her side door and had fed some of the elegant
lunch to Pearl while I waited. When Susan came up the
front stairs from her office at five past one, I had the tape
in the VCR. And the elegant lunch laid out on one of the
upper shelves in her book case, to discourage Pearl.
Susan kissed me, kissed Pearl, and looked at the lunch.

"Is this a submarine sandwich I see before me?" she
said.

"Yes," I said. "No onions."

"Elegant."

When she was working she was much less flamboyant
in her makeup and clothes. "I am not the focus of the
therapy," she said when I once asked her about it. Today
she wore a dark blue pants suit with a white blouse and
pearls. Her makeup was discreet.

"Even if I were sane," I said, "I'd spend $100 an hour
just to come and look at you."

"It's a hundred and a quarter, but I could get you a
rate," she said. She went to the kitchen and came back
with two place mats, knives and forks, and cloth napkins.
She laid out our lunch on the coffee table.

"There's napkins with the subs," I said.

Susan looked at me pityingly, and then turned to glare at
Pearl, who was stalking the sandwiches. Pearl seemed at
ease with the glare, but she didn't get closer. I pointed at the
cassette in the VCR.

"Do you know what's on it?" Susan said.

"Nope, I was waiting for you."

Susan slipped a sliced pickle out of her sandwich and
took a bite of it.

"Roll 'em," she said.

I pressed the play button on the remote control and
there was a moment while the VCR cranked up that the
tape ran for a while with nothing on it, then suddenly

there was Jocelyn Colby tied to a chair with a white scarf over her mouth. She squirmed against the ropes, her eyes, above the scarf, wide with fear. And that was it. The tape ran for about five minutes. There was no sound except the muffled noise she was able to make through the scarf, no message, merely the picture of Jocelyn struggling in captivity. The screen went blank though the tape continued to roll. After it had rolled blankly far enough to persuade me it contained nothing else, I stopped it, and rewound it.

"There was someone," Susan said. "We were wrong."

I nodded.

"How will you find her?" Susan said.

"Let's run the tape again," I said and pressed the play button.

Jocelyn was wearing a black slip and black high-heeled shoes, or more accurately one black high-heeled shoe. The other shoe lay on the floor in front of her. The strap of her slip was off her left shoulder. There was no bra strap. Her ankles and knees were bound with clothes-line. Several loops of the same rope around her waist held her in the chair. The white scarf appeared to be silk. It covered her face from nose to chin. Her dark hair had fallen forward and covered her right eye. In the back-ground of the picture was the corner of a bed. The light seemed natural and seemed to come from Jocelyn's left. Her hands were out of sight behind her back, but from the way she squirmed in the chair it appeared that they were tied to the chair. The chair itself was a sturdy oak straight chair, the kind you find in libraries. The wall behind her was a sort of neutral beige. It was blank.

I ran the tape maybe five more times while Susan sat forward, her chin on her hands, studying it. There was nothing else to see. I shut it off.

"What does he want," Susan said.

"If it's a man," I said.

Susan shook her head impatiently.

"He or she. What does the kidnapper want? Why did he send you this tape?"

"I don't know. It lets me know he's got her."

"There was no letter with the tape?"

"No. Maybe we'll hear something in a while."

"I don't get it," Susan said.

"I think that's my mantra," I said.

"Will you notify the police?"

"Have to. I'll get a copy made of this tape and go to Port City and give the original to DeSpain."

"What else will you do?"

"I'll look into Jocelyn's background a little more. Rummage through her apartment."

Pearl came and put her head in Susan's lap. Susan stroked Pearl's head and turned toward me again.

"I know you value restraint," Susan said. "And I know when you work you try to work with what you know, not what you feel. But it is human to feel bad about this, and it's okay to."

Susan's eyes seemed bottomless. I always felt when I looked at them that my soul could plunge into hers through those eyes and be in peace forever. I leaned over and kissed her on the mouth, and we held the kiss until Pearl reared her head up from Susan's lap and wedged it in between us.

"I have promises to keep," I said and started for the door.

chapter 39

DeSpain and I looked at the tape of Jocelyn's captivity in his office. As he watched, the lines around his mouth deepened. He played the tape twice, and then shut it off. When he looked at me there was something around his eyes that made him look tired.

"You came to me earlier," DeSpain said, "maybe this wouldn't have happened."

"Maybe," I said.

"I'm the Chief of Police in this goddamned town," DeSpain said. His voice was flat. He sounded tired. "I'm supposed to know when a criminal investigation is taking place."

"Didn't want to distract you from your hot pursuit of the theater killer."

DeSpain nodded, tiredly.

"You think there's a connection?" he said.

"Why ask me?" I said. "I didn't even think there was a stalker."

DeSpain nodded again.

"You got the packaging this came in?" he said.

I had it in a big manila envelope. I put the envelope on his desk.

"We'll let the scientists take a look," DeSpain said. "They'll study it and tell me it was mailed in Boston. But that's what we do. We let the fucking crime lab study things." DeSpain shrugged. "Spreads the blame around."

"I was out on Brant Island the other night," I said.

"Yeah?"

"Saw about a hundred Chinese come ashore in a small boat from a big boat."

"You got a subcontract with INS?" DeSpain said.

"Know anything about that?" I said.

"Nope."

We looked at each other. Neither of us spoke. There were no lights on in DeSpain's office. The gray afternoon light came weakly through the rain-streaked window.

Finally I said, "You were a good cop, DeSpain. What the hell happened to you?"

The lines in DeSpain's face got deeper. The eyes got tireder.

"How about you, Sherlock? How good a cop are you? What have you done since you showed up here, except fuck up."

We were silent again. DeSpain didn't seem angry. He seemed sad. There seemed no power left in him, only tiredness.

"So far," I said, "we're about even. Maybe we can recoup by finding this woman."

"I'll find the woman," DeSpain said. Suddenly there was force in his voice as if a switch had been turned on. "You just stay the fuck out of my way."

I stood.

"Sure," I said.

But I didn't mean it. And he knew I didn't, but the force was gone from him as quickly as it had come.

I left and drove over to the theater in my car with Hawk and Vinnie trailing along behind in Hawk's car. There was a light mist coming down, perfect fall weather in Port City. I had the wipers on slow intermittent. I was thinking about Hawk's reaction when I'd told him about Jocelyn. *There was no one following that broad,* he had said. I felt the same way, and it bothered me. I was wrong sometimes, and Hawk was wrong sometimes, but we weren't usually both wrong about this kind of thing. Something else bothered me, and I couldn't find exactly what it was. There was simply something nibbling at the far corner of my consciousness. If I turned toward it, I lost it. If I thought of other things, it was back nibbling. DeSpain was a puzzle too. His reaction was all off. DeSpain was a straight-ahead guy. He wasn't a remembrances-of-things-past kind of guy. He was a get-out-of-my-way-or-I'll-throw-you-in-the-street kind of guy. And then there was the matter if we'd been wrong about Jocelyn's stalker, had we been wrong about Christopholous' stalker. And maybe I hadn't seen illegal Chinese immigrants being smuggled ashore, and maybe this was not Port City I saw but only Asbury Park.

I parked on a hydrant in front of the theater and got out with my duplicate tape and went in. Christopholous didn't have a VCR in his office. He took me to the conference room to view the tape. The VCR and monitor were on a two-level wheeled deal table pushed against the far wall. We sat on a couple of folding chairs in the big empty room under the bright ceiling fixtures with the stylized theater posters marching in endless gallery around the walls and watched, me for about the fifteenth time, as Jocelyn sat helpless in her chair.

"For God sake," Christopholous said when the tape went blank. "What is this?"

"You now know what I know," I said.

"Where'd you get this?"

"Came in the mail this morning," I said. "Postmarked Boston."

"Well, is she what, a hostage? Do they want a ransom? What?"

I shrugged.

"Got any thoughts?" I said.

"Thoughts? Jesus Christ, Spenser, this is your work, not mine. How would I have thoughts. Have you called the police?"

"Yeah."

"Well, that's all I can think of. The theater has no money. If there's a ransom, we have no money to pay it."

"Be nothing left for those nice board member parties if you paid a ransom," I said.

"That's not fair, damn it."

"No, probably isn't," I said. "I'm feeling kind of grouchy about things. You got any kind of personnel file on Jocelyn?"

"I imagine we have her head shot and résumé, Social Security number, that sort of thing."

"Get it for me, will you?" I said.

"Why . . . oh, of course, certainly. Be glad to."

"Now," I said.

"Surely. Excuse me."

Christopholous hustled off and left me alone to sit and stare at the empty room and the myriad posters of things past, without seeing anything.

chapter
40

It was late in the afternoon. I was in my office with about an inch of Irish whisky in the bottom of a water glass and my feet up on the window ledge, looking out. I had searched Jocelyn's apartment and found nothing, except that she appeared to be a neat housekeeper. I had read her folder and learned that she had been born in 1961 in Rochester, New York. I learned that she had studied theater at Emerson College, in Boston. I learned that she had once played Portia in *The Merchant of Venice,* at the Williamstown Theater Festival, that she had done some commercials for a local tire dealer, and that she had been with a theater company in Framingham before she came to Port City. I was closing in fast.

Hawk and Vinnie had gone home. I was willing to risk an ambush by the Death Dragons in exchange for a little solitude. I was sick of being guarded. I was also sick of not knowing what I was doing. It was a common condition for me, but I never got used to it. I sipped my whisky.

Around me in the other offices in the building brief-cases were snapping shut, papers were being filed, drawers were being closed, computers were turning off, copy machines were shutting down. The twenty-three-year-old women who filled the building were restoring makeup, reorganizing hair, reapplying lipstick. The young guys that worked with them were in the men's room checking the haircut, washing up, straightening ties, spraying a little Binaca. Daisy Buchanan's. The Ritz Bar. The Lounge at the Four Seasons. Thank God it's Friday. Children still, most of them, everything ahead of them. Career, sex, love, disaster. All of it still to come, all of it waiting for them while they straightened their ties and smoothed their pantyhose and thought about the first cocktail, and who knew what beyond that. The light dwindled. The street lights along Boylston Street came on. The interior lights of the new building gleamed in repetitious squares across Boylston Street. Once, a while ago, through another window when a different building was there, I used to watch a woman named Linda Thomas lean across her drawing board in the advertising agency that used to be housed there. I swallowed a little more whisky.

It bothered me that whoever had Jocelyn had sent me the tape and nothing else. Why? What did he want? No ransom demand. No threat to do something if I didn't do something. Just a kind of notification. See, I've got her. Maybe it was an orchestrated effort. Let me sweat the picture for a day or so, then send me a letter. Give me a million dollars if you wish to see her alive. Why me? Would I ransom her? The kidnapper had no reason to think I would or that I could. Why kidnap her at all? I had no reason to think she was wealthy. There was nothing in her apartment to make me think that she was wealthy.

I leaned back and got the phone from my desk and called information in Rochester, New York. There were thirty-two Colbys listed. I said thank you and hung up. My glass was empty. I poured another inch or so into it. In one of the offices across the street a young woman was putting on her coat to go home. She shrugged into the coat and then tossed her hair with both hands so that it would fall outside the coat collar. Officially my position was nonsexist. Unofficially, good-looking women were the most interesting thing in the world. I loved the way they moved, the way they canted their head when they put on lipstick, the way they tried on clothes and looked in the mirror, the way they patted their hair, the way their hips swayed when they walked in high-heeled shoes. The young woman across the street looked at herself in the window reflection for a moment, bending forward from the waist, unaffectedly interested in how she looked. Then she stood and turned away, and in a moment the window square went dark.

I picked up my phone again and dialed State Police Headquarters at Ten-Ten Commonwealth Avenue. I asked for Captain Healy and in a moment he came on.

"Spenser," I said. "I need help."

"Glad you finally realize that," Healy said. "Whaddya need?"

"Remember I called you the other day? About an ex-Statie named DeSpain?" I said.

"I remember," Healy said.

"I want you to talk to me about him," I said.

"What's in it for me," Healy said.

"The pleasure of my company," I said. "And a steak at the Capital Grill."

"Steak sounds good," Healy said. "When?"

"Now."

"You're in luck," Healy said. "My wife's going to a movie with her sister, and there's no basketball on."

"So you're desperate."

"Yeah," Healy said. "See you there in an hour."

We hung up. I drank some whisky. Most of the office lights were out across the street. Lights were still on in the corridors, and the offices that the janitors were starting. The desultory lighting made the building seem somehow emptier. My own building was quiet now. There were tequila sunrises being drunk now. Seductions were underway. Healthy Choice frozen entrées were popping into microwaves. The local news people were in paroxysms of jolliness at the anchor desks. Dogs were being walked. I called Susan. She wasn't there. I left an off-color message on her answering machine.

I finished my drink and corked the bottle and put it away in my desk. I got up and washed the glass and put it away. Then I took the Browning off my desk and put it back in its holster on my hip. I put on my coat and turned off the lights and went out of my office, and locked my door.

It was a ten-minute walk from my office to the Capital Grill. I thought about Susan the entire walk and felt much better by the time I got there.

chapter
41

Healy ordered an Absolut martini on the rocks. I did the same. When the waiter left, Healy put a brown envelope on the table in front of me.

"I pulled DeSpain's personnel file," he said. "You have no business looking at it."

"I know," I said.

I picked up the envelope and slipped it into my inside pocket. The waiter returned with the martinis. We ordered food. Healy picked up the martini and looked at it for a moment, then took a drink. He swallowed and shook his head slowly.

"Martinis never disappoint you," he said.

I nodded. Mine was a little less compelling after several ounces of Irish whisky.

"Not many things you can say that about," Healy said.

"Now and then a woman," I said.

Healy nodded slowly.

"Been married thirty-seven years," he said. "You still with Susan?"

"Yeah."

"I remember when you met her. That kidnapping up in Smithfield. She still with the school system?"

"No, she's a shrink," I said.

"You ever get married?"

"No."

"Why not?"

I shrugged.

"Neither of us has wanted to at the same time," I said.

"Live with her?"

"No."

"Makes the time together better, doesn't it?" Healy said.

"Yeah."

"Me and the old lady got separate bedrooms. People are shocked. Think the marriage is in trouble."

"Just the opposite," I said.

Healy nodded. He was a slim man with square shoulders and close-cut gray hair.

"Woulda done it sooner," he said. "But when the kids were home, there weren't enough rooms. Now there are."

He grinned and drank more of his martini.

"Keeps everything fresh," he said.

"Tell me about DeSpain," I said.

"Tell me why you want to know," Healy said.

I told him.

"You do have a touch," Healy said. "Murder, kidnapping, illegal immigrants, and you've managed to annoy the Kwan Chang tong."

"Beats hanging around outside motels with a camera," I said.

"You got backup against Kwan Chang?" Healy said.

"Hawk and Vinnie Morris."

"Vinnie fucking Morris?" Healy said.

"He does what he says he'll do, and he's good with a gun."

"I'll give him that," Healy said. "Never saw anyone could shoot as good as Vinnie."

I said, "Ahem."

Healy ignored me and cut into his steak.

"You want to give me the name of your next of kin?" I said.

Healy grinned.

"My cholesterol is about 150," he said. "I weigh the same as I did when I got out of the Marine Corps."

I looked at my cold seafood assortment. I looked at Healy's steak. I was glad I wasn't eating it. I was glad I was eating cold seafood. Cold seafood was virtuous.

"DeSpain and I started about the same time," Healy said. "He was tougher than a railroad spike, and smart. And stubborn. He got onto a case, he wouldn't let go of it. And he didn't act tough. He was folksy, like Will Rogers. Most people liked him."

The waiter went by, and Healy snagged him, and ordered another martini. The waiter looked at me. I shook my head. Martinis didn't go that well with a cold seafood assortment.

"So he had a big future," I said.

"Yeah. He should have been head of Criminal Investigations by now."

"Instead of you?"

"Instead of me," Healy said. "DeSpain was an investigator for the Middlesex DA, working out of the Framingham barracks. Some sort of stalking situation, and he got himself involved with the victim."

I felt it like a jab in the solar plexus.

"A woman," I said.

"Yeah. How many men you know get stalked?"

"One, maybe," I said.

"Anyway, his marriage broke up, ugly, and it screwed his career. Public Safety Commissioner hates it when we start sleeping with people we're investigating. DeSpain resigned, and I never knew where he went, until you called."

"You don't know the woman's name?"

"No, should be in the file. You think she's involved up in Port City?"

"The kidnap victim, woman named Jocelyn Colby, who claims she was stalked, used to work with a theater company in Framingham."

"Be a big coincidence," Healy said. "This broad up in Port City, she got anything going with DeSpain?"

"Nothing that shows," I said.

"The course of true love," Healy said, "never did run smooth."

chapter
42

I was back and forth between Boston and Port City so much I felt like a carrier pigeon. We were back there again, with Mei Ling, in the Puffin' Muffin, on a rainy Saturday and I was tired of it. I was tired of the drive. I was tired of not working on the house in Concord. I was tired of the rain. I was tired of being about a step and a half behind. I was tired of not seeing Susan. I was tired of Hawk and Vinnie following me around. I missed Pearl.

"Hawk, you and Mei Ling work Chinatown. Door to door, anybody who'll talk. Vinnie, you do the waterfront."

"And the Death Dragons?" Vinnie said.

"Screw the Death Dragons," I said.

"Do you really think this is the way to find Miss Colby?" Mei Ling said.

"No," I said. "But it's the best I can think of."

"Gimme Vinnie," Hawk said.

I stared at him. I'd never heard him ask for help.

"I want somebody looking out for Missy," he said. "Case I have to beat up the Death Dragons."

"Never thought of that," I said.

"I know," Hawk said.

"I am not afraid," Mei Ling said.

"I know," I said. "Vinnie?"

"Sure," Vinnie said. He was eating a pumpkin muffin.

"Okay, I'm going over to the theater, ask the same people the same questions, again. We can meet in the theater lobby at noon. Compare notes, see who's found out the least."

Hawk smiled widely.

He said, "Nice to see you so upbeat."

"If you see any Death Dragons, shoot them," I said. "I'm tired of them too." They got up and left, Mei Ling walking close beside Hawk, her head not nearly level with his shoulder. I paid the bill and went to the theater and began again to round up the usual suspects.

At ten minutes to twelve I was in the big empty conference room with Deirdre Thompson and her chest, which she kept pointing at me. She was wearing jeans and a powder blue tee shirt that advertised the Casablanca Restaurant. The neck of the tee shirt had been cut with scissors into a low scoop that bared most of her shoulders, and barely maintained itself over her cleavage.

"Jocelyn ever express a romantic interest in Christopholous?" I said.

"Oh, hell," Deirdre said. "Probably. If you've got a testicle, Jocelyn will sooner or later express a romantic interest."

"Nicely put," I said.

"Yeah, well, she's a piece of work," Deirdre said. "God, I hope you can get her back."

"Do you remember whether she specifically was interested in Christopholous?" I said.

"You think he's grabbed her?" Deirdre said.

I took in some air and let it out, slowly.

"No. Did she?"

"Yeah. One of the things about Jocelyn. She likes, ah, men, who, ah, . . ." Deirdre made a kind of rolling gesture with her hands. "Authority figures. That's what I was trying to say. She's hot for authority figures."

"Like Christopholous."

"Sure. She was hot for Jimmy for a while. But he wasn't interested. Don't tell him you got this from me, okay?"

"Okay."

"Everybody knew about it and I think it embarrassed him. Hell, nobody thought anything about it, you know? Like, that's Jocelyn. She's a hell of a lot of fun, you know, so you just buy the package—the men, the drinking, the mess in the dressing room, we all got quirks."

"A mess in the dressing room?"

"Yeah. Like that's a clue?"

"Tell me about that."

"Well, you ever see a theater dressing room, it's not usually like in the movies." She grinned and pantomimed fixing her hair in a mirror, and did a stage manager voice. "'Five minutes, Miss Garbo.' You know. It's like the changing room at a discount store. Everybody's jammed together, in their skivvies, getting out of one thing and into another. It's a mess, and if someone is sloppy, it's that much more of a mess. It is, in fact, a pain in the ass.

But Jocelyn . . ." Deirdre shrugged. "She could never keep it neat. She's clean, and she's neat about herself, but she's a slob. You should see her place."

"Her apartment?"

"Yeah, looks like the day after the last day of Pompeii: bed's a jumble, clothes everywhere, makeup on the floor. It's hysterical."

"What would you think if you went in there and found it neat?"

Deirdre laughed.

"I'd think her mother came for a visit. Except I know her mother's dead."

"Father?" I said.

"Father took off when she was a little girl," Deirdre said. "I don't think she ever heard from him. I don't think she knows if he's dead or alive. And she says she doesn't care."

I nodded.

"Maybe she does," I said.

chapter
43

At lunch we compared findings.

"Nobody in Chinatown will talk to us," Hawk said.

"You feel it's a racial thing?" I said.

"Naw," Hawk said. "I think they seen me with you."

I nodded. Mei Ling was looking approvingly at Hawk. Vinnie was spreading cream cheese on a bagel. He seemed entirely relaxed, but as always, no matter what else he was doing, he was looking around the room.

"According to one of her friends, Jocelyn had a crush on Christopholous."

"Which he hasn't mentioned to you."

"Correct. And according to her friend, she was a legendary slob."

"So?"

"So when I searched her room it was ready for inspection."

"Who the friend?" Hawk said.

"Deirdre Thompson."

"Our Lady of the Boobs," he said.

Mei Ling blushed slightly and giggled.

"You think maybe Jocelyn cleaned up her room because she knew it might be searched?"

"Maybe," I said.

"Do you mean to say she knew she would be kidnapped?" Mei Ling said. She looked as outraged as it was possible for Mei Ling to look. Which was not very.

"Maybe," I said. "Would you be willing to gain illegal entry to Jocelyn's apartment with me?" I said to Mei Ling.

She looked startled and then looked at Hawk.

"He want you to look, 'cause you a woman," Hawk said. "Might see things he didn't."

"I hope you don't find that sexist," I said.

Mei Ling smiled.

"No, sir," she said. "Women often see things that men have missed."

"Good," I said. "Let's go."

Mei Ling looked at Hawk again.

"Will you come with us?"

"Drive you over, Missy. Wait right outside."

I left enough money on the table to cover lunch. Vinnie lingered a moment while he made a cream cheese sandwich with his second bagel, wrapped it in a paper napkin, and stuck it in his pocket.

"Be glad when this is over," he said. "Go someplace and get some actual, fit for human consumption, chop."

Jocelyn had a basement apartment, down three concrete stairs on the side of a three-story clapboard building near the water. There was a black pipe railing on the stairs, and heavy screening on the windows. The door was painted black.

Since I had already done it once before, it took me about a minute to jimmy the lock. The room was as I'd left it. If DeSpain had gone through it, he'd done it neatly. There was a bed sitting room, a kitchen and a bath. The bath was tiled. The other two rooms were finished in plywood paneling. There was a pink satin spread on the bed.

"You should look around, Mei Ling. See if anything appears odd. Anything that should be here and isn't. Anything that is here and shouldn't be. Anything you don't expect."

Mei Ling stood in the middle of the room and looked around.

"May I open drawers and closets and things?"

"Yes."

She did. She was quite organized about it. She began at the far end of the bed sitting room and moved methodically through it and the kitchen and finally the bath. I leaned on the wall near the kitchen counter and watched her as she worked. Her face was serious, and a small concentration wrinkle appeared vertically between her eyebrows. Her front teeth showed as she bit down gently on her lower lip while she carefully looked at everything.

"Her makeup is not here," Mei Ling said. "Neither is her purse."

"It would make sense," I said, "for her to have her purse when she was kidnapped. Is it reasonable to imagine that she would have kept her makeup in her purse?"

"Is this an attractive woman?" Mei Ling said. "An actress, one who cares about her appearance?"

"Yeah."

"Then, no, sir. She would have had lipstick in her purse, and maybe blusher and a little something to touch up her eyes. But she would not have carried everything in her purse." Mei Ling smiled. "There is too much. Her bathroom is not well lighted. There is no window. She would have had a magnifying mirror, perhaps one with built-in lighting. She would have had a hair dryer. She would have had night cream, and moisturizer, and foundation, and eye shadow, and mascara, and . . ." Mei Ling spread her hands helplessly. "So much. And besides, her whole organizer is gone."

"A makeup organizer?"

"Yes."

"You know she would have one?"

Mei Ling smiled at me almost condescendingly.

"Yes, sir."

"Anything else?" I said.

"I don't know what she had for luggage," Mei Ling said. "But there is no suitcase."

"Yeah," I said. "I noticed that too, but at the time it wasn't what I was looking for."

"Her tooth brush and tooth paste are still here," Mei Ling said.

"Yeah. But a lot of people keep an extra already packed."

"What does this mean, sir?"

"Maybe Jocelyn packed for her kidnapping," I said.

"Who would let her do that?"

"Nobody," I said.

chapter
44

I was alone in Port City. I needed to think, and I was beyond caring whether the Death Dragons and Lonnie Wu liked it or not. The sky was dark, the wind was brisk off the Atlantic, but the rain was gentle, drifting a little on the wind. I walked along Ocean Street, parallel to the water, away from the theater, with the collar up on my black leather jacket and my matching White Sox baseball cap pulled down over my forehead. I had the Browning out of its holster and in my right-hand coat pocket, because if the Death Dragons did, in fact, protest my presence, it would be embarrassing if my gun was out of the rain, dry and cozy, zipped up under my jacket. Most of the fishing boats were in harbor, and their masts clustered near the shore, bobbing briskly on choppy water the color of macadam, the herring gulls roosting on them and on the pilings along the piers. One of them planed off its perch and snatched a piece of garbage from the sullen water. The thing that had been skittering intangibly along the edges of my consciousness coalesced suddenly. Like a name I'd been trying to think of.

I turned and went back to the theater, walking fast; in the front door, past the box office, up the stairs and into the big empty conference room galleried with theater posters. I walked straight to the one advertising the Port City Theater Company's 1983 production of *The Trials of Emily Edwards.*

Neatly framed. One of fifty, it was a stylized portrait of a young woman with black hair tied to a chair and gagged with a white scarf. She was wearing a black slip and black high-heeled shoes, or, more accurately, one black high-heeled shoe. The other shoe lay on the floor in front of her. The strap of her slip was off her left shoulder. There was no bra strap. Her ankles and knees were bound with clothesline. Several loops of the same rope around her waist held her in the chair. The white scarf appeared to be silk. It covered her face from nose to chin. Her dark hair had fallen forward and covered her right eye. It was identical to Jocelyn's predicament on the tape. She had learned how to kidnap herself, by copying a play poster.

"Jesus Christ," I said. It came out very loud in the empty conference room.

I took the poster off its hook and with me as I left the theater. Nobody stopped me. No one said, "Hey, boy, where you going with that poster?" No one, in fact, paid any attention to me at all. *If a detective falls in the forest,* I thought, *does he make a sound?*

I took the poster to my car and drove home to Susan's. When I got there, I went quietly with my poster past her waiting room. For a moment I thought of going in. *Excuse me, doctor, but I think I need vocational counseling.* Instead I went on upstairs. I put my hat on her hall table so she'd see it when she came up from her afternoon appointments and not be startled when she came in. I let myself in to Susan's apartment with my key, accepted, with considerably more grace than pleasure, three minutes of intense lapping from Pearl, then took my coat off and made myself a double vodka martini on the rocks with a twist. I put my poster on top of the TV, put the video tape in the VCR, clicked play, waited until Jocelyn was on the screen, and clicked the freeze-frame button. Freeze frame was not state of the art on Susan's VCR, but it was sufficient. Then Pearl and I got on the couch and looked at the likeness while I sipped my martini and thought about the detective business. Pearl made an occasional attempt on my martini, which I repelled. After a couple of failures she gave up and turned around twice and lay down with her head on the arm of the couch and her butt against my leg.

I had been in Port City now, with three employees, since, approximately, the time that Hector was a pup. And the only fact I had was that Craig Sampson had been shot dead in front of me on the stage at the Port City Theater. The only person in Port City who had told me anything useful was Lonnie Wu, who had threatened to kill me, and even he had exaggerated. Though in defense of Lonnie, I was harder to kill than he had expected.

My drink was gone. I got up to get another one. Pearl turned her head and looked at me with annoyance. I made a shaker of martinis and came back and sat again. Pearl sighed and rearranged herself once more.

"Yeah," I said to her. "I know."

I stared at the two images. Jocelyn must have set her video camera on a tripod and then sat in her chair and tied the scarf over her mouth. She could then have tied her ankles and knees together, looped the rope through the chair rungs, wrapped it around her waist and held it behind her with her unbound hands. It would enable her to struggle realistically, and to make muffled sounds through the scarf, and set herself free by simply letting go of the rope behind her and then untying her legs. She could have done all this with the tape running and then gone into her bound-and-helpless act for five minutes or so and then erased the tape up to the point she'd started her act.

I poured another martini and raised my glass toward Jocelyn on the screen.

"All the world's a stage, Jocelyn," I said.

I looked at Pearl.

"A tale told by an idiot," I said. "Full of sound and fury, signifying nothing."

Pearl looked at me without moving her head.

"I know they're lines from different plays," I said to her. "But Jocelyn probably doesn't."

I heard Susan's key in the door. Pearl exploded off the couch, put one hind foot in my groin, and dashed at Susan as she came in.

Susan said something to her that sounded like "fudding wuddying pudding," but maybe wasn't, and came on into the living room and gave me a kiss.

"Martinis," she said, and looked at my eyes. "And more than one."

I nodded toward the television and the poster. Susan turned and stared at them. It didn't take her long.

"For God's sake," Susan said after less than a minute. "She's faked her kidnapping."

"And all the people merely players that fret and strut their moment upon the stage."

"You've mixed two plays," Susan said.

I looked at Pearl.

"See," I said. "She's smarter than Jocelyn."

chapter
45

The first thing I saw when I woke up was Susan's pink and lavender flannel night gown in a heap on the floor. This was an excellent sign. I peeked under the covers. Susan was naked except for a pair of thick white athletic socks. This was another good sign. Susan normally slept in thick flannel from late August until mid July. She wore the socks all year. On her night table was a half-empty martini glass. I thought back over the night. My memory of the night, though furtive, confirmed the evidence of the morning. Susan, apparently on the basis of if-you-can't-lick-'em-join-em, had jumped into the martinis with me and we had talked of everything but Port City, and eaten spaghetti late, and gone to bed and the flannel night gown had ended up on the floor. I looked at Susan; she had the covers up over her nose and her eyes open, looking at me.

"What are you going to do?" she said.

"After I get us some orange juice, I'm going to fondle your naked body until you are racked with desire," I said.

"I *know* that," Susan said. "I mean what are you going to do later, about Jocelyn."

"I don't know. Should I find her?"

Pearl pushed her nose through the nearly closed door and wiggled the door open and came into the bedroom. She jumped up on the bed and looked at the covers until I held them up, then she snaked down under them, in between us, and went to sleep. Susan patted her.

"How will you do that?" Susan said.

"She probably went to a motel," I said. "If you're going to kidnap yourself, it may make the papers; you can't stay with a friend."

"But wouldn't she use a false name?" Susan said.

"She'd need a credit card, and she probably doesn't have any false ones," I said.

"So you'll just check area motels?"

"Yeah."

"And unless she had a bunch of cash, you'll find her."

"And if she had a bunch of cash, someone will remember her for that," I said.

"It's harder to hide than one might think," Susan said.

"Especially for amateurs. But should I find her? She has almost certainly staged this to get my attention."

"Yes," Susan said. "But we don't want her to keep escalating what she does until she gets your attention."

"Good point," I said.

We drank some orange juice and fooled around a little and then Susan looked at the clock, and rolled out of bed.

"My God," she said. "My first appointment comes in an hour."

She began to speed about her bedroom while I lay in bed and watched her.

"Why not start a little earlier?" I said. "So you don't have to dash around?"

"Because I was being grabbed by a hyper-gonadic thug," Susan said as she stared into her closet. She was the only person I knew who could ponder hurriedly.

"Happen to you often?"

"Fortunately, yes."

Susan took out a jacket, studied it frenetically, and threw it on a chair. She took out another jacket, held it against herself and looked in the mirror.

"Maybe that would look better," I said, "if you were wearing something on the bottom."

"The guys at the health club tell me just the opposite," Susan said.

"They may have a point," I said.

But she didn't hear me; she had zoomed into the bathroom and closed the door. I finished my orange juice and got up and put on my pants and let Pearl out and fed her. I heard the shower running. I went back to the bedroom and made the bed. The blue pinstripe suit that Susan had chosen for the day hung neatly on hangers from a hook inside the closet door. The things she had discarded were scattered around the room like autumn leaves the west wind fleeing. I heard the shower stop. I hung the clothes back up on their hangers. In the closet the clothes were carefully separated so as not to wrinkle. I never figured out her neatness rules. Whatever they were, they were suspended while she dressed. I took the martini glasses to the kitchen and put them in the dishwasher along with the plates and pans from last night's supper. Then I made some coffee.

I was on my second cup when Susan emerged from the

bathroom naked with her hair done and her makeup on. I took coffee into the bedroom while she dressed.

"What are you going to do?" she said.

"I guess I'll see if I can find Jocelyn."

"Could we be wrong?" Susan said. "Could someone else have copied that poster when they tied her up? And she really is a captive?"

"We could be wrong," I said. "But we're probably not. If I find her, we'll know."

Susan nodded.

"So we go with our best guess," she said.

"Don't you?" I said.

"In therapy? Yes, I suppose so, guided by intelligence and experience, and something else."

"What else?" I said.

"I hate the word," Susan said, "but, intuition?"

"Whatever," I said. "You use a little science and a little art."

"Yes."

"Me too," I said.

"And rather well," she said. "Could you snap this for me?"

I did. When she was gone, and the air still eddied with her scent, I took a shower and dressed and turned on CNN for Pearl to watch while she was alone, and went to my office.

First check the mail, then find Jocelyn.

chapter
46

When I got there, Rikki Wu was sitting on the floor in the
hall outside my office door. She had her knees pulled up
to her chest and her face buried in her folded arms. When
I stopped in front of her, she looked up and her eyes were
red from crying. Some of her eye makeup had run. I put
down a hand and she took it, and I helped her to her feet.
I held her hand while I unlocked my door, and led her
inside, and put her in the chair in front of my desk. Then
I went around and sat in my chair on the other side of the
desk and leaned back and looked at her.

"What do you need?" I said.

She hugged herself a little and shivered.

"Would you like some coffee?" I said.

She continued to hug herself and shiver. She nodded
her head slightly. I got up and put coffee in the filter and
water in the reservoir and pushed the button. Then I came

back and sat down. Neither of us spoke. The coffeemaker muttered. Rikki continued to hug herself and stare at nothing. The coffeemaker subsided, and I got up and poured some.

"Milk?" I said. "Sugar?"

"Milk," she said in a small voice. "Two sugars."

I brought her coffee, placed it on the edge of my desk in front of her. I took mine and went around and sat down again. She picked up the coffee cup with both hands and sipped some coffee. Her lipstick made a bright crescent on the edge of her cup.

"I don't know who else," she said.

"Un huh," I said.

"There's no one I can trust."

I nodded.

She sipped her coffee again and raised her eyes from the cup and looked straight at me for the first time since I'd arrived.

"Can I trust you?" she said.

"Yeah," I said. "You can."

"My husband's gone."

"Gone?"

"They've taken him. I know he's dead."

She drank some more coffee, holding the mug with both hands carefully. The mail I had come to check was in a pile on the floor near the mail slot.

"Tell me about it," I said.

Rikki pressed the coffee mug against her cheek as if warming herself.

"My husband always stayed in his office at the restaurant until ten o'clock. Then he would have one scotch and soda at the bar, and come home. Two of the boys would drive him."

"Death Dragon boys?"

"Yes. Last night he did not come home at ten. I called his office. There was no answer. I called the restaurant. My husband had left early, alone. He told the boys to wait there for him, that he would be back. The boys were still there waiting. He did not come back."

"Why do you think he's dead?"

She shrugged.

"If he were not, he would have come home. They have killed him."

"Who?"

"They. The people my husband did business with."

"Do you know any names?" I said.

She shrugged again.

"I did not know about my husband's business. It was not my place to know. But it was a business where a person could be killed."

"Have you been to the police?" I said.

"No. I do not trust the police."

"Why not?"

Rikki shook her head.

"I do not trust them," she said.

"But you trust me," I said.

"Yes."

"Why?"

"I do not know," she said. "But I do."

I was hoping for a bigger endorsement than that, but one takes what's there.

"How about the Dragons?"

"I don't trust them either."

I nodded.

"Would you like me to come up to Port City with you," I said, "and help you find your husband?"

"Yes."

I nodded. So much for checking the mail. Or looking

for Jocelyn. Now I could look for Lonnie. I wondered if his disappearance had to do with Jocelyn's disappearance. Maybe they were sitting in a motel room together, pretending to be kidnapped. This wasn't working like it was supposed to. The more I investigated, the more I learned, the less I understood. I was having trouble even keeping track of who my client was. Was I working for Christopholous, or the Port City Theater Company, or Jocelyn Colby, or Rikki Wu? Or Susan? Since no one was paying me it was kind of hard to be sure.

"Okay," I said. "Let me make a call."

I pulled the telephone over and called Hawk.

"Who we been looking for?" I said.

"Jocelyn?"

"Yeah."

"And there someone there so you being cagey."

"Yeah. I think things are not as they appear to be. I think the person is in a motel in the area. Voluntarily."

"She faked it?"

"Yeah."

"So she be in a motel under her own name," Hawk said. "'Less she got lot of cash."

"Un huh. You and Vinnie see you can find her," I said.

"She could be with somebody else," Hawk said.

"If she is, find them too," I said. "Don't do anything. Just locate her and let me know."

"Sure. You going to the movies?"

"Lonnie Wu is missing," I said. "His wife is here in the office. I'm going to help her find him."

Hawk was silent for a long moment on the phone.

"Maybe Lonnie with Jocelyn," he said after a while.

"Maybe so," I said.

Hawk was quiet again.

Then he said, "This the silliest thing you ever got me involved in."

"Without question," I said.

"Maybe the Death Dragons won't bother you," Hawk said. "You with Mrs. Wu."

"I'm not worried about the Death Dragons," I said. "At least I know where I stand with them."

"No small thing," Hawk said, "in Port City."

chapter
47

It was the gang kids that found Lonnie Wu. In the bird-watching pavilion out across the causeway on Brant Island Road, where I had stood in the darkness watching the ghostly Asians immigrating. When Rikki and I got there, only two of them were around, leaning against a black Firebird with chrome pipes and silver wings painted on the hood. Neither one looked old enough to drive. They spoke to Rikki in Chinese and nodded toward the pavilion. She took my arm as we walked toward it.

Lonnie was there. Crumpled in the corner, his back propped against the low railing, his feet stuck straight out in front of him, his argyle socks looking forlorn. You don't have to have seen many corpses to know one when you see one. I heard Rikki's breath go in sharply and felt her hand tighten on my arm.

"No need to look," I said.

She didn't answer, but we kept going until we were standing right above him, looking down. He was facing west, his back to the ocean, and the early afternoon sun hit him full in the face. Before Lonnie died, someone had beaten hell out of him. His nose was broken, one eye was closed. His lip was so swollen it had turned inside out, and several of his teeth were missing. There was dark blood soaked into the front of his shirt. Rikki stared down at him for a moment, then turned away and pressed her face against my chest. I put my arm around her. Several herring gulls swept in on the wind and settled on the pilings of the causeway, reorganizing their feathers as they landed. Road kill was road kill to them. They didn't make fine distinctions.

"Do you have a friend that you could stay with?" I said to Rikki Wu.

With her face still pressed against my chest, she shook her head no.

"Family?"

"My brother will come."

"Okay," I said. "I'll ask you to sit in the car for a minute or two and then we'll go back together."

She made no reply, but she didn't resist when I turned her and walked back to the Mustang. The two kids looked at me blankly. They made no finer distinctions than the gulls.

"Either one of you speak English?" I said.

The smaller of the two wore an oversized Chicago Bulls jacket. He smiled widely. The other one, taller but just as frail, with his long hair blown forward by the wind, showed no expression at all.

"Dandy," I said and went back up the causeway. I heard the doors open and close on the Firebird and then it started up and roared away. Who could blame them. No reason to hang around. They didn't work for Lonnie Wu anymore.

I squatted on my heels beside Lonnie's body. I didn't like it, but there was no one else to do it. I felt inside his coat and found his holster on his belt near his right hip. The holster was empty. I looked for bullet holes or stab wounds. I saw none. I felt along his rib cage, I could feel some broken ribs. In one instance the fracture was compound. I felt myself grimace. Some of his fingers appeared broken. His flesh was cold, and he was stiff. His hair was tangled, and strands of it, stiffened by hair spray, stuck straight out at odd angles. He was so messed up it was hard to tell for sure, but probably the gulls had already been at him.

I stood and looked down at Lonnie's body. He was as far from China as he could get, on the eastern edge of the wrong continent, on the western edge of the wrong ocean. I looked out at the waves rolling uneventfully in from the horizon. They came a long way to this shore, but not as far as Lonnie had come, and nowhere near as far as he had gone.

I turned away and walked back down to my car and got in beside Rikki. She wasn't crying. She simply sat staring at nothing, her face composed, her hands folded in her lap. I started the car and let it idle.

"We should call the cops," I said.

"No," Rikki said. "I will call my brother."

"Eddie Lee?"

"Yes. He will take care of everything."

"The body?"

"Everything."

"So why didn't you call him in the first place?" I said. "Why did you come to me?"

"I didn't want him to know," she said. "I didn't want him to know that my husband was gone. I didn't know what we'd find out. My brother doesn't, didn't, admire my husband. He thought he was shallow and vain. I didn't want to shame myself."

"Your husband got to be the *dai low* here because he married you," I said.

"Yes."

"Might the tong have killed him?" I said.

"No. My brother is my brother. He would not allow anyone to kill my husband."

"Even if he were disloyal to Kwan Chang?"

"My brother would not allow someone to kill my husband."

"Someone killed him," I said.

"It was not a Chinese person," she said firmly.

I nodded and handed her the car phone. She dialed and spoke in Chinese while I turned the car and headed back toward town. When Rikki got through I called Mei Ling.

chapter
48

Two silent Chinese women had come to sit with Rikki Wu at her home, and I was alone with Fast Eddie Lee and Mei Ling in the office behind the restaurant. It was a small room with a rolltop desk and a computer on a roll-away stand. On the wall above the rolltop was a picture of Chiang Kai-shek in his generalissimo suit, the tunic buttoned tight at the neck.

Eddie was a solid old man, not very tall, but thick, with a round face and blunt hands. He had wispy white hair and there were liver spots on the bare scalp that showed through. He was wearing black pants and a white shirt, and he sat on Lonnie Wu's leather swivel chair with both feet flat on the floor and his hands resting on his knees. He looked at me without any expression for a while.

"You have the body?" I said to him.

He nodded.

"You speak English?" I said.

"Some," he said. "Better Chinese." He turned his head slowly and looked at Mei Ling. She smiled and spoke in Chinese. He answered her briefly and then turned his head back slowly to look at me some more.

"You know what killed him?" I said.

He nodded. He spoke to Mei Ling.

"He says his doctor has examined Mr. Wu," Mei Ling said. "He was beaten to death."

I nodded.

"Where's the body now?" I said.

Eddie Lee looked at Mei Ling. She translated. He answered.

"He says the body is being properly cared for."

I nodded again. Eddie and I looked at each other some more. Mei Ling sat beside me on a hassock, her knees neatly together. She was perfectly quiet. The only light was the green-shaded desk lamp behind Eddie Lee. I felt like somewhere there ought to be a guy playing a gong.

"And the cops?"

Eddie spoke to Mei Ling.

"He says this is not police business. He says it is Kwan Chang business," she said.

"It's my business too," I said.

Mei Ling translated. Eddie listened and then looked at me again.

"No," he said. "Chinese business."

"I understand how you feel," I said. "It's not only Chinese, it's family."

Mei Ling translated.

"But you need to understand me. I am a detective. It's what I do, and what I do is pretty much who I am."

I waited for Mei Ling. Eddie listened without any response.

"So somebody gets shot in front of me, and me being a detective and all, I figure I should find out who did it."

Mei Ling translated. Fast Eddie listened. He was in no hurry. As far as I could tell he had forever.

"And I can't. I get threatened, and shot at, and lied to, and bamboozled. There are stalkers and not stalkers and connections I don't know about. There's a kidnapping that maybe isn't, and all I get is bewitched, bothered, and bewildered."

I paused for Mei Ling.

"I do not know how to translate bamboozled," she said.

"Hoodwinked," I said.

She translated. Fast Eddie smiled. With his thinning white hair and placid bearing, he looked like a pleasant old man. I knew he wasn't. He spoke to Mei Ling.

"He says he feels sorry for you. He understands how frustrating it must be. He thanks you for helping his sister."

I nodded.

Fast Eddie spoke again.

"But you would do well to leave the killing of Mr. Wu to him," Mei Ling said.

I shook my head.

"No," I said. "I'm going to find out what's going on here."

Mei Ling and Fast Eddie talked for a moment.

"He says you appear to be a hard man."

"Tell him it takes one to know one," I said.

Mei Ling spoke. Eddie Lee listened and smiled. He looked at me.

"Yes," he said. "It does."

Eddie took a package of Lucky Strikes out of his shirt pocket and shook one loose from the pack and stuck it in his mouth. He lit it with a Zippo lighter. Then he put his hands back on his knees and looked at me. He would take an occasional drag on the cigarette and exhale without taking the cigarette from his mouth. Otherwise he was motionless.

"I know about the immigrant smuggling," I said.

Mei Ling translated. Eddie took the news calmly.

"So?" he said.

"So here's the deal." I said. "You stop smuggling the people in. I don't say anything to the INS. I keep rummaging around until I know what the hell is going on down here. You put a lid on the Death Dragons. I keep you informed."

Mei Ling translated. Fast Eddie sucked in some cigarette smoke and let it out. The ash was growing long on his cigarette.

"Why should I deal?" he said to me.

"Because it's a lot easier than trying to take me out."

Mei Ling translated. Eddie Lee smiled again, one eye squinting as the smoke from his cigarette drifted past.

"You think be hard to kill you?"

"Yeah," I said. "Be hard."

Eddie Lee dug another cigarette out of his pocket and lit it with the butt of the first one, dropped the butt into a small vase filled with sand, and left the new cigarette smoking in the corner of his mouth. Then he looked at me and spoke in Chinese. I held his look and when he finished Mei Ling translated.

"He says he is a sensible man," Mei Ling said. "He says he recognizes that killing you now would cause trouble among your friends, some of whom are police. He says this does not mean he can't kill you, but that he has decided not to for now. He says the smuggling of people will not end. But it will end in Port City. And he says if you keep him informed, and do not cause any trouble, you may continue to investigate. No Chinese people will interfere with you."

"Does he know anything that can help me?" I said.

Eddie Lee shook his head before Mei Ling could translate.

"You know anything about a woman named Jocelyn Colby?"

Eddie Lee had to wait for Mei Ling on this. The name probably confused him. When she finished translating, he shook his head.

"Ever hear the name?"

He shook his head.

"Was DeSpain in Lonnie's pocket?" I said.

"Yes," Eddie Lee said.

"But you don't want him involved in the case?"

Eddie Lee looked at Mei Ling. She translated. Eddie Lee shook his head.

"Chinese business," Eddie Lee said. Then he smiled suddenly. "And you," he said.

chapter
49

Hawk was wearing a white leather trenchcoat and aviator sunglasses and leaning on his car when I met him in the parking lot of the Holiday Inn at Portsmouth Circle, just south of the bridge over the Piscataway River. On the other side of the bridge was Maine. It was cold near the water and Hawk had his collar turned up as he leaned on the white Jaguar.

"Ran a little farther than we thought she would," I said.

"She on the second floor, in the back," Hawk said. "Vinnie's watching the room from out back. Only other way out is through the lobby and out that door."

"Have any trouble with the desk clerk?" I said as we started toward the lobby.

"Naw. Been watching you close. I think I learning."

"Sometimes the desk clerks are hard to get around," I said.

We went into the small lobby. The dining room was to the right. The desk straight ahead. Behind the desk was a good-looking young black woman, wearing large hoop earrings. She smiled very brightly at Hawk. He nodded at her.

"And sometimes they're not," I said.

On the second floor, Hawk said, "Number 208, down here on the right."

"You got a pass key?" I said.

Hawk grinned and produced one.

"'Course I do," he said.

"What did you tell her?"

"The sister at the desk? Told her she was the most exciting woman I ever had," he said.

"And?"

"Told her you was my boss and it was your first wedding anniversary and you wanted to set up a nice surprise for your wife."

"And you needed a key to set it up."

"Un huh."

"And then you mentioned again how she was very important to you."

"Un huh."

"This smacks of sexist exploitation," I said.

"Do," Hawk said, "don't it."

We reached 208. Hawk put the key in the lock.

"She got the chain on, we'll hit it together," I said.

Hawk nodded, turned the key, and pushed. The door opened five inches and held against the chain.

"Who is it," a woman said.

Hawk straightened and stepped back.

"On three," I said. "One, two, three."

We hit the door together. Hawk with his left shoulder, me with my right, and the chain lock tore out of the door jamb, and the door flew open, and slammed against the wall, and we were in the room with Jocelyn.

I closed the door behind us.

Jocelyn Colby, wearing jeans and an oversized tee shirt, was sitting on the bed propped against the pillows with the television on and a copy of *Elle* magazine open on her lap. She stared at us with her mouth open. I walked past the bed to the windows and looked down and waved Vinnie up from the back parking lot. Then I turned and rested my hips against the window sill and crossed my arms and looked at Jocelyn.

"We've come to your rescue," I said.

Jocelyn continued to stare with her mouth open. Then she closed it, and swung her feet to the floor.

"Oh, thank God you're here," she said.

She stood and pressed herself against me and wrapped her arms around my waist. I looked at Hawk. He grinned.

"Want me to step outside?" he said.

The door opened as Vinnie came in. He had his Walkman earphones around his neck. When he looked at me, he seemed even more amused than Hawk.

"You getting laid?" he said.

"Vinnie," I said. "You got the soul of a poet."

"Longfellow," Vinnie said, and chuckled to himself. Hawk liked it.

"Longfellow," he said. And he and Vinnie both laughed.

Jocelyn appeared not to notice. She pressed against me with her head on my chest and her arms tight around me.

She kept murmuring, "Thank God, thank God, you've found me."

I assumed she was stalling while she tried to think up a story.

I looked past her around the room. It was motel standard: beige walls, double bed with a beige spread, bureau with television on it, bathroom and closet in an alcove, bedside table with a beige phone, straight chair.

"One of you poets mind checking the closet and the bureau," I said, "see if you can find a clue?"

Still happy with the Longfellow remark, both of them looked. Hawk went into the bath/closet alcove, and came out with a video camera on a tripod. Vinnie searched the bureau and came up with a black slip, a white silk scarf, and about twenty-five feet of clothesline. Hawk picked up the straight chair, placed it before the blank wall next to the doorway, opposite the window. He put the video camera on its tripod a few feet in front of it. Vinnie draped the black slip and the white scarf over the back of the chair, and put the coiled rope on the seat.

"Jocelyn," I said.

She buried her face harder against my chest. I took hold of her upper arms and separated myself from her and held her away from me at arm's length.

"Jocelyn," I said. "Cut the crap."

She started to cry.

"Okay," I said. "Good. Now raise your tear-stained face and gaze beseechingly into my eyes."

She stepped away from me and looked at all three of us. I took the opportunity to get my butt off the window ledge and stand upright.

"One woman," she said, "and three men. And the men standing around laughing. Isn't that typical?"

I didn't know how typical it was, so I let it slide.

"Don't you realize I've been through hell," she said.

"You may have gone through hell, Jocelyn, but you weren't kidnapped."

"I was," she said. She was crying harder now, though it didn't seem to impede her speech.

Hawk went into the bathroom.

"Nope," I said. "You checked yourself in to this motel with your own credit card. You videoed yourself tied to the chair, you even copied a theater poster when you did it, though you may not know it."

Jocelyn took one step back and sat hard on the edge of the bed. Hawk came out of the bathroom with a handful of Kleenex. He handed them to Jocelyn. She took them without paying any attention and held them crumpled in her hand.

"Tell me about it," I said.

"What's the use," she said, with the tears rolling down her face. "You don't believe me, anyway."

"You were the one stalking Christopholous, weren't you?" I said.

She buried her face in her hands and cried louder. Now in addition to tears, there was boo-hoo.

"You had a crush on him, and he didn't respond, and so you began to follow him around."

She turned and lay on the bed and buried her face in the pillow and sobbed.

"We got time, Jocelyn. We got nowhere to go. When you're through crying, you can tell me."

She cried louder and buried her head deeper into the pillow. I waited. Hawk was leaning on the wall watching Jocelyn, the way you'd watch an interesting but not very affecting movie. Vinnie had his arms folded, leaning against the door, looking out the window across the room. His earphones were back over his ears. He was listening to music. Jocelyn's fists were tightly clenched, the unused Kleenex still held in her right fist. She began to pound on the mattress as she cried. Then she kicked her feet. The crying began to wear down after a time. The pounding stopped and the kicking became desultory. She began to moan, "Oh God, oh God" and twist on the bed as if she were in pain. And finally that stopped and she lay still, her face still in the pillow, as her breathing began to normalize. She needed more air so she took her head out of the pillow and turned it away from us, toward the window. The room was quiet.

"So how come you kidnapped yourself?" I said.

I could see Jocelyn thinking about my question and thinking about her answer, and I could see her body go almost limp in a kind of physiological surrender.

"You wouldn't believe me," Jocelyn said. Her voice was shaky. "I had to convince you that I needed help."

"Help with what?" I said.

"Oh, God," she said.

"We all need help with him," I said. "What else."

"It's what . . ." she paused and struggled with her breath. ". . . it's what every woman needs."

"The love of a good man," I said. I was falling into her speech patterns.

"Yes," she said. The final sibilant came out in a long hiss. "You were everything I ever wanted, but you had *her!*"

The way she said *her* sounded like she might have been speaking of Vlad the Impaler.

"Susan," I said.

"Yes. *Susan. Susan, Susan, Susan.* There's always a goddamned *Susan.*"

"What a drag," I said. "DeSpain have a Susan?"

Her whole body stiffened. She turned her head toward me and rolled over on her side and looked at me as if I had spoken in tongues.

"DeSpain?"

"Yeah. Didn't you and he have a fling in Framingham? About ten years ago? You were with the Metro West Theater Group. Somebody was stalking you. He was the investigating officer."

Jocelyn sat up on the edge of the tangled bed. Her eyes were red and puffy, her face was lined with the fabric of the bedspread. She patted at her hair, trying to get her appearance back into line.

"I can barely recall the incident," she said.

"Even though the same DeSpain is now Chief of Police in Port City, where you are working and living when not tying yourself up in hotel rooms?"

"It's something I've put behind me. It was a long time ago and it was very distasteful."

"He was married, wasn't he?"

"Yes. To a hideous travesty of womanhood."

"And he left her for you."

"He wanted me, he needed me."

"So what happened?"

"What do you mean?"

"How come you and DeSpain aren't cheek by jowl ever after?" I said.

She frowned.

"I told you," she said. "It's over."

"He turned out not to be everything you ever wanted? He was a pig?"

I waited. She looked at me and past me and past Hawk and Vinnie at things that none of us had ever seen. She took in a deep breath and let it out in a long sigh.

"I wanted love," she said. "He wanted sex."

"That combo would never work," I said.

"No."

I waited again. She didn't elaborate.

"So how come you both ended up in Port City?" I said.

"I came here to work," she said.

"And DeSpain?"

"You'll have to ask him."

"Who was stalking you in Framingham?" I said.

"I was working part-time at a child care center," she said. "My supervisor was stalking me."

"They convict him?"

She laughed. It was a surprising laugh, guttural and humorless.

"The old boy system doesn't convict its kind," she said.

"Must be a glitch somewhere," I said. "Lots of guys doing time."

"You know what I mean," she said.

"Sure."

We were quiet. The day had dwindled into late afternoon. The motel window, facing east, looked out on a darkening parking lot. There were no lights on in the room except the lamp by the bed and its small yellow illumination served only to make the rest of the room look grayer.

"Tell me about Christopholous," I said.

"It's not like you think it was," she said.

I didn't say anything. Her voice seemed steady; and, though still quite small, gaining strength. I realized she was beginning to warm to her performance. Alone, in the center of three men's attention, she was beginning to like it.

"We were mad about each other," she said. "It was all we could do to keep from falling into each other's arms in public."

"Why shouldn't you fall into each other's arms in public?" I said.

"He wanted me passionately," Jocelyn said. "And I loved him more than life itself."

"But now you don't?"

She paused for a long time.

"It's over," she said finally.

"Because?"

"Because he found someone else," she said.

"Another Susan," I said.

Jocelyn nodded so slowly, as to be ponderous.

"Exactly," she said. "Another goddamned Susan."

"You knew her?"

Jocelyn shook her head.

"But it had to be someone else, didn't it?"

"He adored me," she said, "until some bitch got her claws into him."

"So you had to follow him around, see who it was."

Jocelyn nodded vigorously.

"And to be near him. To be able to look at him even if only from afar. To be there for him if he ever needed me."

"Nothing wrong with making him a little uncomfortable, the sonovabitch," I said.

"The bastard," Jocelyn said.

"Ever find out who the Susan was?" I said.

"I never caught them," Jocelyn said. "But I had my suspicions. The way they talked together, the way she looked at him. How she'd leave early from a board meeting or come late to a show case. And he wouldn't be

in his office, the way she wasn't always where she said
she'd be. I had my suspicions."

My heart felt like a stone in my chest. I saw where we
were going.

"Rikki Wu," I said.

"Absolutely," Jocelyn said. "She had her hooks into
him down to the bone."

"So you made an anonymous call," I said.

She looked a little surprised.

"Like the kind you made to Susan about me," I said.

She looked more surprised.

"You called Lonnie Wu and hinted his wife was
fooling around."

"She had to be stopped," Jocelyn said. "He was
everything I ever wanted."

The phrase was like a password. Her eyes were bright
and her face had a mild flush to it. The tip of her tongue
trembled on her lower lip. A lot of *he's* had been
everything she ever wanted. I wasn't even sure she knew
who this *he* was as she spoke.

"Jesus Christ," Hawk said behind me.

Without turning I nodded *yes.*

"So Lonnie looked into it and found out you were
right. His wife was fooling around, but not with Christopholous. Who was she balling, Hawk?"

"Craig Sampson," Hawk said behind me.

"Bingo," I said.

"So Lonnie send one of the kids up," Hawk said, "and
had him sloped."

"Just as he launched into a chorus of 'Lucky in
Love,'" I said. "Lonnie must have liked the symbolism."

"Better than Sampson did," Hawk said.

The room was quiet. The three of us stood looking at
Jocelyn. Outside there was no more daylight. In the

darkened room only Jocelyn's face was lit by the bedside lamp. I looked at it for a long time. Pretty in a blurred sort of way, not leading-lady looks, someone to play the maid, maybe, the gangster's girlfriend. Not very old, not very smart. Innocuous, mostly empty, an idle face upon whose blank facade life had etched no hint of experience. She had noticed nothing tangible. She had lived a life of clichéd fixations. If she felt anything about the way things had worked out, she didn't feel it very deeply. Even her obsessions seemed shallow . . . She heaved a slow sigh.

"You know what's so tragic?" she said. "After all I've done, all I've been through, I'm still alone."

I didn't say anything. There wasn't anything to say. I just looked at her vapid, empty, uncomprehending face, bottomless in its self-absorption, a monster's face.

"Get your stuff together," I said to Jocelyn. "We're going."

She seemed to shake herself from a reverie for a moment, and stared at all of us in the dark room as if she hadn't known we were there. Everything she did seemed done in front of a camera. Vinnie went to the closet and took out her suitcase and opened it on the bed for her. He pointed at it. She made a pulling-herself-together shrug as she stood up and began to gather her things.

"You got a thought on who pounded Lonnie?" Hawk said. In the darkness he was an invisible presence still leaning motionless on the wall.

"Yeah."

"And you don't like it much."

"No."

"Not too many choices left," Hawk said.

"Not many," I said.

"So we be going up to Port City again," Hawk said.

"Yeah."

"What we going to do with Norma Desmond?" Hawk said.

"We'll bring her along. Maybe she'll be useful."

"Sure," Hawk said. "There a first time for everything."

chapter
50

I was in the Port City Police Station, in DeSpain's office with the door closed. DeSpain looked red-eyed and raw sitting behind his desk. He tipped his head forward and began to rub the back of his neck with his left hand.

"I found Jocelyn Colby," I said.

He stopped rubbing but kept his head tipped forward.

"She all right?" he said. His voice sounded hoarse, as if he had brought it up from a dark place.

"She's not hurt," I said.

"Good."

We sat silently for a time. DeSpain still looking down, his left hand motionless on the back of his neck. There was light from the squad room drifting in through the pebble glass door to DeSpain's office. And the green-shaded banker's lamp was lit on his desk. So the room

wasn't dark. But it was shadowy, and felt like offices do
at night, even a cop office.

"She faked the kidnapping," I said after a while.

DeSpain thought about that for a moment, then he
looked up slowly, his left hand still on the back of his
neck, the thick fingers digging into the muscles at the
base of his neck.

"Oh, shit," he said.

"Exactly," I said.

I reached into my inside pocket and took out the
envelope that Healy had given me containing DeSpain's
file. I tossed it on the desk between us. DeSpain looked
down at it, at the Department of Public Safety return
address. He picked it up, slowly, and took his hand away
from the back of his neck, slowly, and opened the
envelope, slowly, and took out the file, and unfolded it,
and read it, slowly. We were in no hurry, DeSpain and I.
Port City was eternal and there was no reason to rush.
DeSpain looked carefully at the photocopy of his record
with the state police, at the copy of the sexual harassment
complaint filed by Victor Quagliosi, Esq. on behalf of
Jocelyn Colby, which was attached. He read, though he
probably could recite it, his letter of resignation, also
attached. When he was through, he evened the papers
out, folded them carefully back the way they had been,
and put them in their envelope. He slid the envelope back
across the desk toward me. I took it and put it back in my
pocket. DeSpain leaned back in his swivel chair and
folded his arms and looked straight at me.

"So?"

"You want to talk about Jocelyn?" I said.

"What's to say?"

"She's crazy," I said.

"Yeah," DeSpain said and his voice still seemed to rumble up from a place far down. "She is."

I didn't say anything. DeSpain looked at me. There were deep grooves running from the wings of his nose to the corners of his mouth. I could hear his breath going in and out, slowly. He unfolded his arms, and rested his chin on his left hand, the elbow on the chair arm, the thumb beneath the chin, the knuckle of the forefinger pressed against his upper lip. He puffed his cheeks and blew small puffs of air past his loosely closed lips.

It made a small popping sound.

"She was crazy when I met her," DeSpain said. "Only I didn't know it. She doesn't seem crazy, you know."

"I know."

"I was married," DeSpain said. "Grown kids. Wife drank a little, liked a few belts before supper, got out of hand sometimes at parties, but we got along. Then this little broad comes in with a stalker story and I'm working investigations and I catch it."

DeSpain shook his head. In the shadowy room his eyes seemed simply dark recesses, buried beneath his forehead.

"And . . . Jesus Christ. She feels my muscle, she wants to see my gun, she wants to know if I killed somebody, and what was it like, and would I take care of her, and she leaned her little tits on me and looked up at me, and I never had anything like it happen to me in my life. Second night on the case we're in bed and she's a volcano. The old lady did it in her flannel night gown, you know? With her eyes shut tight."

"What about the stalker?" I said.

"The case was bullshit," DeSpain said. "Guy wasn't stalking her. She made a pass at him and he turned her down and she made it up."

"That didn't warn you?" I said.

"If she shot me in the belly it wouldn't have warned me," DeSpain said. "I couldn't get enough of her."

"So you ditched the wife."

"Yeah. Don't even know where she is now. What happened to her. Kids won't talk to me."

He paused for a moment and leaned back. He pressed his hands together and looked at them as if they were new, and then began to rub them slowly together, leaning back as he spoke, so that all I could see of him now was the hands rubbing slowly together in the lamplight.

"Child-care supervisor, the one she said stalked her, he threatened to sue her for defamation, so I went up and knocked him around a little, you know, to discourage him, and the bastard got a lawyer and went right to the C.O."

"The bastard," I said.

"Yeah, well C.O. got him calmed down. Made some sort of settlement that didn't get all over the papers, and I had to go. C.O. liked me, but he had no choice."

In the darkened room DeSpain's voice sounded as if he were talking through a rusty pipe.

"But you still had Jocelyn," I said.

"Yeah. Except as soon as I moved in with her . . ." he shrugged. "She lost interest. Told me I was just an animal, just after sex like some kind of dirty animal. Came home one day and she was gone. No note, no thanks-for-the-memories."

"You weren't forbidden fruit anymore," I said.

"Sure," DeSpain said. "But I still knew how to be a cop. I found her easy enough. So I come up here too. C.O. knew some people here. They needed a chief. C.O. gave me a plug."

"To be near her."

DeSpain didn't say anything. In the lamplight his hands were now still. Behind him through the window I saw small lightning shimmer across the sky. It was so far away that I never did hear the thunder.

"And Lonnie Wu?" I said. "When did you hook up with Lonnie?"

"I never bothered her," DeSpain said.

He leaned forward now, his face back in the lamplight, his thick hands, still pressed together, resting on the desk top.

"I'd go see her sometimes in one of those asshole fucking plays she was in," he said. "She couldn't act for shit. But I never went near her. Just liked knowing where she was, being around, maybe, if she needed help or anything."

"Lonnie?" I said.

"Fucking gook," DeSpain said. "Was smuggling in Chinamen. Been going on a long time. People on the hill that owned the mills, when the mills folded, moved into fish processing, and needed cheap labor."

"So most of the smuggled Chinese stayed here?"

"At first, then the fish plant jobs filled up. So Lonnie would smuggle in a few replacements for people who died, or saved up enough to get out, or got killed for not making the trip payments on time. And the rest he would funnel into Boston, and the tong would place them."

"Kwan Chang," I said.

DeSpain nodded.

"Lonnie was Fast Eddie Lee's brother-in-law," I said.

"I knew he was wired," DeSpain said.

"And he paid you not to see the smuggling."

"Yeah."

"You know who killed Sampson?" I said.

"Yeah."

"You know why?"

"He was fooling around with Rikki Wu."

"You know how he found out?" I said.

"Jocelyn told him," DeSpain said.

"You know why she told him?"

"Probably after Sampson," DeSpain said. "I never cared."

"She was after Christopholous," I said. "She thought Rikki was in the way."

DeSpain was silent for a time.

"So, right broad, wrong guy," he said finally. "Why'd she fake the kidnapping?"

"To get my attention," I said.

"She was after you?" DeSpain said.

"It was my turn."

DeSpain rocked back in his chair and sat, his body slack, his arms limp, his hands inert in his lap. He didn't speak. I didn't either. Behind him the lightning flickered again, and, distantly after it, some thunder, not very loud.

"You thought Lonnie took her, didn't you?" I said.

DeSpain didn't say anything.

"You figured since she'd told him about Sampson, then she'd know Lonnie did it, and he wanted her quiet."

DeSpain still sat looking at nothing at the edge of the lamplight.

"I figured she was squeezing him," DeSpain said. "Be her style."

"And he wouldn't just kill her?"

"He knew about me and her. He knew he couldn't get away with killing her. I figured he took her and was going to negotiate something with me."

"So you went and got him and dragged him out to Brant Island and tried to make him tell you where she was," I said.

DeSpain was motionless and silent.

"Except, of course, he didn't know," I said.

The lightning flashed outside, shining for a strobic moment on the black-and-whites parked in the lot, and the thunder came, much closer behind it now, and rain began to rattle on the glass in DeSpain's window.

"So you beat him to death," I said.

DeSpain thought about that for a long time, his hands perfectly still in the circle of light on the desk top in front of him.

"Yeah," DeSpain said finally, "I did."

chapter
51

It was raining hard now, and the water was washing down DeSpain's window in thick, silvery sheets when the lightning flashed.

"You got her with you?" DeSpain said.

"She's with Hawk," I said, "and Vinnie over at the Muffin Shop."

"I'd like to see her."

"Use your phone?" I said to DeSpain.

He nodded toward it. I stood and picked it up and called Healy.

"I think you better come down here," I said to Healy. "Port City Police Chief has confessed to murder. I'm in his office."

"I want to see her," DeSpain said.

I nodded as Healy was talking.

"Healy wants to speak with you," I said.

DeSpain shook his head.

"Won't talk to you," I said into the phone. "We'll be in a place called The Puffin' Muffin, in the arcade at the Port City Theater."

DeSpain was on his feet when I hung up, and starting for the door. I followed along. Which was pretty much what I'd been doing since I came to Port City, just following along, about ten steps back of whatever was really going on. DeSpain went through the station without a word for anyone, and out the front door and down the steps. The rain was hard, and resentful when we walked into it. We turned left on Ocean Street and headed for the theater. I had on my leather jacket and White Sox baseball hat. DeSpain was bare-headed, without a coat. The rain glistened on the handle of his service pistol, stuck on his belt, back of his right hipbone. His hair was plastered to his skull before we had gone five steps. He didn't seem to mind. My jacket was open and my shirt was getting wet, but I didn't want to zip up over my gun.

Jocelyn was facing the door as we walked in. Hawk was beside her and Vinnie was at the counter getting coffee. There were five women at the other end of the room drinking coffee, shopping bags on the floor beside them. A boy and a girl, high school-aged, were near the door. As we came in, Hawk leaned back a little in his chair so his coat would fall open. At the counter Vinnie put down the coffee cup and turned to look at us. He stood motionless, his coat open, his shoulders relaxed. The pink-haired waitress in her cute uniform looked at DeSpain nervously and walked rapidly back down to the other end of the counter.

DeSpain walked directly to Jocelyn and stopped. She looked at him the way you'd look at a dirty sexual animal. He looked at her face a moment as if he were seeing someone he thought he knew but wasn't sure about. Hawk glanced at me. I made a little let-it-go hand gesture. Hawk looked back at DeSpain.

"You murderous little cunt," DeSpain said and slapped her hard across the face. The slap knocked her sprawling out of her chair and onto the floor. Hawk stood and stepped between them.

"Get out of my way," DeSpain said.

Hawk was motionless.

"DeSpain," I said.

He tried to step past Hawk and Hawk moved in front of him again. I stepped in close behind him.

"DeSpain," I said.

Outside the lightning crashed and the thunder was simultaneous. DeSpain looked back at me. Then he looked at Hawk and turned suddenly and stepped away from all of us. He had his hand near his hip.

"I had to do that. It was worth my life to do that," he said.

Jocelyn had stayed on the floor, lying on her side, her face blank with shock, blood coming from her nose.

"Now it's done," I said.

"Healy coming?" DeSpain said.

"He's sending some people from the Topsfield Barracks."

DeSpain nodded. His face was still wet with rain, his hair dripping wet, his soaking shirt stuck to his body. Suddenly he smiled, the old wolfish smile.

"Goddamn, I liked that," he said. "She had that coming, and one hell of a lot more."

"I got no argument with that," I said. "But I can't let you do it again."

"Don't matter," DeSpain said. "Once was all I needed."

He grinned at me.

"You think you can hold me here for Healy?"

"Yeah," I said. "I think we can."

DeSpain slowly reached back and unsnapped the safety strap on his holster. The smile was wider, more wolfish. The voice was strong again, and the eyes, still deep in their sockets, seemed almost to glow.

"Let's find out," DeSpain said. "I'm walking. Anyone tries to stop me, I'll shoot him."

"There's three of us, DeSpain. That's suicide."

"Yeah." DeSpain's grin was wide. "Maybe you never seen me shoot."

He moved toward the door, I moved in front of it and DeSpain pulled his gun. He had it half out of the holster when Vinnie shot him. Four shots in the middle of the chest, so fast it seemed one sound. DeSpain went backwards three steps, sat slowly, and fell over on his back, the front sight of his pistol still hidden in the holster. I looked at Hawk. He and I hadn't cleared leather. I let my gun settle back in the holster and went and sat on my heels beside DeSpain. I felt his neck. There was no pulse. I looked at his chest. Vinnie had grouped his shots so you could have covered all four with a playing card. I looked over at Jocelyn; she was sitting upright now, still on the floor, hugging her knees. Her eyes were shiny, and her tongue flittered on her lower lip. I stood up. Vinnie had put the gun away. He picked up his cup and sipped some of his coffee. Everyone else in the restaurant was flat on the floor.

"It's all over, folks," I said. "State police coming."

Nobody moved. I looked at Vinnie.

"Quick," I said.

Vinnie nodded.

"Very," he said.

Hawk reached down and hauled Jocelyn to her feet.

"The animal," she said softly. "He hit me. I'm glad he's dead."

"Shut up," Hawk said.

Jocelyn started to say something and looked at Hawk and stopped and was silent. I stood and stared down for a while at DeSpain. One of the toughest guys I ever met. I looked over at Hawk. He was looking at DeSpain too.

"The short happy life," I said, "of Francis Macomber."

chapter
52

I had the last French window into the new addition on the Concord house when Hawk's Jaguar rolled into the driveway on a bright blue day in November with no wind and temperatures in the forties.

"I got lunch," Hawk said as he got out of his Jaguar and went around and opened the door for Mei Ling. "We been to Chinatown and Mei Ling ordered."

"No chicken feet," I said. "We don't do chicken feet."

"American people are quite strange," Mei Ling said.

She was carrying a very large shopping bag. Pearl the Wonder Dog, ever alert, homed in on it at once, sniffing furiously. Mei Ling looked nervous.

"What kind of dog is that?" she said.

"Pearl don't like being called a dog," Hawk said.

He scooped Pearl up in his arms and let her lap his face

for a while until Mei Ling had gotten the food into the house.

It was too late in the fall now to eat outside, so the picnic table was inside, in a space that would one day be a dining room. Susan and Mei Ling cleared the hand tools off of it, and spread the blue tablecloth over it and began to set out the Chinese food. Hawk went to the refrigerator, which was next to the table saw, and opened it and took out two long-neck bottles of Rolling Rock. He handed one to me and we stood out of the way drinking it. Hawk was dressed for the country. Black jeans, white silk shirt, charcoal brown tweed cashmere sport jacket, and cordovan cowboy boots.

"You just come from a tango contest?" I said.

"Me and Mei Ling been, ah, recuperating from our Port City ordeal."

"Lunch," Susan said.

We sat. Pearl moved about the table, looking for an opening. We had paper plates and passed the many cartons around. It was an exotic assortment of Asian cuisine, not all of which I recognized. Hawk and I drank some beer. Susan and Mei Ling had wine. I suspected that the workday had ended.

"What will happen to Jocelyn?" Mei Ling said.

"Not enough," Hawk said.

"Can they charge her with filing a false report to the police?" Susan said.

"On the kidnapping?"

"Yes."

"No. All she did was send me a tape of her pretending to be tied up. Healy's working on some kind of conspiracy rap with the DA up there, but they're not sure it'll hold water."

"She was responsible for three deaths, one way or another," Susan said.

"Yeah," I said. "She went through Port City like a virus."

"At least you stopped the illegal immigrant smuggling," Mei Ling said.

She was sitting beside Hawk on the picnic table bench. She sat very close to him and looked at him all the time. He smiled at her.

"Didn't stop it. Just got it relocated," he said.

"Of course, this is true, all Chinese people know what can change and what cannot," Mei Ling said.

"So she may get away with it."

"She may," I said.

I gave Pearl a pork dumpling, and one for me. I drank some beer.

"Of course," Susan said, "while punishment would be satisfying, what she really requires is treatment."

"She's not likely to seek it," I said.

"Then she'll do more damage," Susan said.

"Maybe Vinnie shot the wrong person," I said.

Susan looked at me solemnly for a moment, thinking about it.

"American people too," Susan said and smiled at Mei Ling, "have to know what can change and what cannot, I guess."

"Maybe I can get her to come and talk to you," I said.

"I hope so," Susan said.

"And maybe I can't."

"As long as you keep coming around, Tootsie," Susan said. "That will do fine."

Mei Ling took a shrimp dumpling off of her plate with chopsticks and offered it to Hawk. He opened his mouth and she plopped it in. Pearl watched this closely and went and put her head on Mei Ling's lap. Mei Ling looked a little scared but took another shrimp dumpling and fed it to Pearl. I looked across the table at Susan and felt the heaviness of Port City begin to ease.

"Yeah," I said. "That will do fine."

If you enjoyed

walking shadow

then don't miss Robert B. Parker's exciting new Spenser thriller

thin air

A beautiful woman vanishes, leaving Spenser to probe the mysteries of her checkered past—a masterful work of detection that leads him on a trail of obsession and violence . . .

Available in hardcover from G. P. Putnam's Sons

Turn the page for a sample of this thrilling new work . . .

He had brought several silk scarves with him in a shopping bag, and had used them to gag her and to bind her hands and feet.

"The silk is gentle," he had said to her. "It will not cut you as rope would."

Now she lay helpless, full of fear and anger at her helplessness, on a mattress in the back of an old yellow Ford van while he drove. As he drove he played with the radio until he found a country western station.

"Here it is, Angel—90 FM, Rock Country, remember?"

If she raised her head, Lisa could see through the front windshield. The tops of trees went by, and poles and power lines. No buildings. So she wasn't in the city now.

"God, how long's it been, Lees? Ten months and six

days. Nearly a year. Man, it's been a hard year . . . but now it's over. We're together."

The van hit a pothole and Lisa bounced uncomfortably on the mattress on the floor of the van. The gag in her mouth was soaked with her saliva; she knew she was drooling a little.

"And that's all that matters," he said. "Whatever happened, happened, and it's over. Now it's all ahead of us. Now we're together."

The van had slowed. They were in traffic. She could hear it, and the van braked often, making her slide around on the mattress. It seemed like a brand-new mattress. Had he bought it for this? Like he'd bought the silk scarves? The van halted altogether. Through the windshield she could see the cab of a trailer truck beside them. If she could only wriggle forward a little maybe the truck driver would see her. But she couldn't. He had looped a rope through her bound ankles and tied it to a ring in the van floor. She was anchored where she was. Traffic started again. The radio played, he sang along with it. The traffic stopped. He turned while they were standing, and aimed an ancient video camera at her over the seat.

"Got to get this on tape, our first time together again."

She heard the camera whir.

"Look up, Angel, at the camera."

She buried her face in the mattress. The camera whirred for another moment. Then it stopped and the van started up again.

I was hitting the heavy bag in Henry Cimoli's Harbor Health Club. The fact that there was a heavy bag to hit was largely out of loyalty to me, and to Hawk, and to Henry past. He had owned the place since it was an ugly gym where fighters trained, having once been a ranked lightweight until Willie Pep urged him into the health club business by knocking him out in the first round of both their fights. It was a lesson in the difference between good and great. Joe Walcott had once taught me the same lesson when I was very young, though it took me longer to learn it.

Outside the boxing cubicle which Henry had squeezed in next to his office was a Babylon of glass and chrome and spandex, where personal trainers, mostly young women with big hair, wearing shiny leotards, trained people on the politically correct way to tone up and be better. Many of them viewed me with suspicion. Henry said it was because I looked like I was there to repossess the equipment.

Henry shmoozed among them with a white silk tee shirt stretched over his upper body, looking like Arnold Schwarznegger writ small. He had no shame. When I complained to him that he'd turned the club into a dating bar for the overemployed, he just smiled and rubbed his thumb across his first two fingers. Only if business was slow and he thought no one was watching would he come into the little boxing room and make the speed bag dance. On the other side of Henry's office was a hair salon and a place that gave facials. Upstairs they did aerobics.

I was mainly doing combinations on the heavy bag to keep my hands, wrists, and forearms in shape. I still had to hit people now and again, and I didn't want to hurt myself in the process. I was doing left jab, left jab, right cross, duck, when Frank Belson came in. He had the build for the place, narrow and hard with a thin face. But the tweed scally cap wasn't right, and the tan wind-breaker wasn't right, and the permanent blue shadow of a beard that no razor could eliminate wasn't right. No matter what they do, cops finally end up looking like cops. Or crooks, which is why they do well under cover.

"I need to talk," Belson said.

I stopped, breathing hard, my shirt wet with sweat. The opposite end of the room was a full picture window that looked out over Boston harbor. The water was choppy today and scattered with whitecaps. The big airport shuttle from Rowe's Wharf moved serenely across the inconsequential chop. There was nothing else moving in the harbor except the gulls.

"Sure," I said.

"Somewhere else," Belson said.

"Private?"

"Private."

Henry was talking to a plump woman with frizzy blonde hair who was trying to do half pushups with the motivational support of her trainer, a sleek young woman with purple tights and a big purple bow, who kept saying things like "excellent" and "you can do it."

"Liz, I've already done eight," the blonde woman said.

"Six," Liz said. "But whatever's comfortable."

I gestured at Henry. He saw me and nodded.

"You're doing terrific, Buffy," Henry said to the blonde. "And it's really beginning to show."

The blonde woman smiled at him as she rested from her six or eight half pushups. Henry turned and walked toward me.

"You're doing great too," he said.

"Yeah, it'll show soon. You know Frank Belson."

Henry nodded.

"We've met."

Belson said, "Henry."

"Can we use your office for a while," I said. "Frank and I need to talk."

"Go ahead," Henry said. "I got at least another hour of kissing ass and telling lies before lunch."

"That's called doing business, Henry," I said.

"Yeah. Sure." He looked at me solemnly. "And have a great workout," he said.

Belson and I went into his office and closed the door. I sat in Henry's chair behind his desk. Belson stood, looking out through the glass door at the flashy exercise room. I waited. I'd known Belson for more than twenty years, since the days when I was a cop. He had in that time never asked to speak with me alone, and on any other occasion I could think of would have taken the seat behind the desk. He turned back from staring at the exercise room and looked at the wall behind me. I knew, without looking, because I'd been there often, that there were four or five pictures of Henry when he boxed and at least two pictures of Henry in his current incarnation smiling with celebrated Bostonians who worked out at his club. Belson studied the pictures for a while.

"Henry a good fighter?" he said.

"Yeah."

Belson looked at the wall some more as if memorizing every picture was something he had to do. He put his hands in his hip pockets as he studied the pictures. I leaned back a little in Henry's swivel chair. My breathing had regularized. I felt warm and loose from the exercise. I put my feet up on the desk. Belson stared at the pictures.

"My wife's gone," he said.

"Where?"

"I don't know."

"Why?"

"I don't know."

"Has she left you?" I said.

"I don't know. She's gone. Just disappeared. You know?"

Belson kept his gaze riveted on Henry's wall.

"Tell me about it," I said.

"You know my wife?"

"Yeah, sure. Susan and I were at the wedding."

"Her name's Lisa."

I nodded.

"Second wife, you know."

"Yeah. I know that, Frank."

"And she's a lot younger, and too good looking for me, anyway."

"You think she left you," I said.

"She wouldn't do that. She wouldn't go off without a word."

"You think something happened to her?"

"I checked every hospital in New England," Belson said. "I got a missing person report on the wire all over the northeast. I called every cop I know personally, told them to look out for her. They'll pay attention. She's a cop's wife."

He turned and stared out at the exercise room again. Henry's office was silent.

"She could take care of herself. She's been around."

"You and she been having trouble?" I said.

His back still to me, he shook his head.

"You want me to look for her?"

He was motionless. I waited. Finally he spoke.

"No. I can do that. We don't find her soon, I'll take time off," he said. "I know how to look."

I nodded.

"What's her maiden name?" I said.

"St. Claire."

"She got family somewhere?"

Belson turned and looked straight at me for the first time.

"I don't want to talk about it," he said.

I nodded. Belson stared out at the people exercising in their variegated spandex. Sometimes I thought it was like golf; people did it so they could wear the clothes. But then I noticed that most people looked funny in the clothes and decided I was wrong. Or most of them knew themselves but slightly. The silence in Henry's office was stifling. I waited. Belson stared.

Finally, I said, "You don't want to talk about it, Frank, and you don't want me to help you look, how come you came here and told me about it?"

He stared silently for another time, then he spoke without turning.

"Happened to you," he said. "Ten, twelve years ago."

"Susan left for a while," I said.

"She told you she was going."

"She left a note," I said.

Belson stared silently through the window. The exercisers were exercising, and the trainers were training, but I knew Belson wasn't looking at them. He wasn't looking at anything.

"She came back," he said.

"So to speak," I said. "We worked it out."

"Lisa didn't leave no note," Belson said.

Anything I could think of to say about that was not encouraging.

"When I find her I'll ask her about that," he said.

He turned finally and looked straight at me.

"Thanks for your time," he said and went out the office door.

It was dark when the van stopped. She could hear a radio playing somewhere and a dog barking. He got out of the car and came around and opened the van doors. She wriggled into a sitting position. The camera light was bright in her eyes. The camera whirred.

"Look at me, honey," he said. "We are home now . . . No, look this way . . . turn your head . . . come on, do not be such a tease."

Behind him a short man appeared pushing a hand truck with a tarpaulin over his shoulder. The camera continued to whir.

"Just give me a minute . . . I want to get everything . . . you don't get it and then later you are sorry . . . wait until we have children, I'll be behind this camera all the time."

The whirring stopped. "Okay, Rico," he said, "take her up."

With a buck knife, Rico cut the rope that anchored her to the floor of the van. He picked up her purse from the floor of the van and hung it over one handle of the hand truck. Then he pushed her flat and rolled her in to the tarp. He heaved her onto the hand truck, strapped her to it, and wheeled her away. She could see nothing. The tarpulin smelled of turpentine and mildew. She heard a door open and felt the hand truck begin to bump up some stairs. She jostled on it like a sack of potatoes. It was what she felt like, a helpless, inert, jostling sack of Lisa. The frame of the hand truck hurt her as it dug into her side. She couldn't complain. She couldn't speak. It was too much. She couldn't bear it. She could feel her breath slipping in and out, feel the sweat soaking her clothing, feel the saliva-soaked gag in her mouth. The hand truck bumped and then slid along smoothly and then began to bump again. She twisted futilely inside her canvas and tried to scream and couldn't.

NEW IN HARDCOVER

ROBERT B. PARKER

a spenser novel

SMALL VICES

PUTNAM